NOLA BLUES

By Cara M. King

Dedication

This book was a long time coming.

Shout out to: Tony P. who believed in my creative quest and taught me about the New Orleans bar business when I was 20. Patrick K. who also admired me for following my dreams. Adamz because he told me he believed in me years ago. Marcie for paving the way to Tulane! Nicole O., my friend and party partner at Tulane who I thought of as I wrote Jackson. Total opposites, however she embodied her fun spirit. She held my hand when we were in an accident, and I had to have stitches in my head. I wished I could have held her hand while she battled cancer. She passed at age 37. My grandmother for telling me from beyond this world that she liked my heroine and the twists and turns. Mom and Dad for sending me to Tulane. At least the $120,000 paid for this book. BRich and Baby Cole. Lastly, to those that lost their lives due to the regime of Pablo Escobar.

Table of Contents

Chapter 1

December 1998

My heart beat fast as I dialed the number. I waited. I punched in the special code, my social security number, at the prompt. I thought the automated telephone voice was joking as it announced my big fat D.

Maybe it said B as in boy. I couldn't tell, and I succumbed to hitting the button a third time. Best two out of three. I waited a second and when the automated voice spoke, I imagined it yelled at me, "D as in dumb."

I hung the phone up and shook my right leg, anxiously tapping my bare foot on the cheap blue floor that felt more like cardboard than carpet. Couldn't they at least put padded carpet down? We paid enough for tuition. My roommate, Jackson Milton, kept asking them to put in that expensive Berber carpet.

Jackson was from Manhattan and her parents made their wealth in liquor and nightclubs all the way back from the time of Prohibition. They conceived her at the grand opening of their first Mississippi nightclub, but she didn't have a speck of southern in her. Except, maybe when her ex-boyfriend Cyrus was screwing her.

I grabbed my book bag and headed out of my dorm room. Although my last hope was out of my control, I had to try. I practically ran across campus. The few people who stood in my way quickly moved as I passed with my book bag swinging from left to right. I headed up the steps to the University building that housed my professor's office. I hoped she hadn't left for winter break already.

I knocked on the door labeled Professor Hynes. She wasn't the easiest person to talk to. Have you ever had that one difficult teacher? The class was already hard enough and she made it worse by talking softly, so you had to strain to hear. Her material was poorly organized, and she didn't provide good examples.

She also had a burn on her face, and I felt nervous whenever I spoke to her. Like somehow my unblemished white skin, long brown hair, brown eyes and height of 5 foot 7 created my own Scarlet Letter.

"What can I do for you?" She snapped. *As if she didn't know.* "I was just leaving for my vacation." She seriously needed a lesson in social skills. I was surprised she had even made it past the Dean for hiring.

I had faced tougher opponents than her. Growing up in foster care, nothing was ever black or white. The experience made me a colorful person. The people surrounding me had been ones who altered their state of mind or scammed their surroundings for their own self-gratification, not to mention ephemeral pleasure.

Come to think about it, maybe some of these people still surrounded me in the form of frat boys, however they had a viable excuse for their misdeeds.

I realized early in foster care that I was going to have to take care of myself, so no one was of much consequence to me. It all changed in college. Professor Hynes made me nervous because my future depended on her.

"The grade reporter system says I have a D, and I can't take a D. I'll lose my scholarship." My voice quivered slightly and my tone changed to sound bossy instead of pleading to cover my perceived weakness of crying.

Professor Hynes began to sort through a huge pile of exams and flashed the C I earned. "Unfortunately, you didn't score high enough on the final to raise your grade. I'm sorry." I didn't get that impression since she held the paper close to me like I needed glasses.

"Can I do extra credit, please?"

"You asked me already. The answer is still no. It wouldn't be fair to let you do extra work and no one else."

"Did they ask?"

"You should have taken an "I" when you knew you weren't doing well." An "I" stood for incomplete, but I thought it stood for *incompetent.*

"Your class will keep me below a 3.0. I was on probation this semester because I received below a 3.0 last semester. I'll lose my scholarship money. I won't be able to come back to school next semester. Loans don't come through that fast and my scholarship is ten thousand dollars a semester. I thought I could raise the grade. You know I tried. I asked questions during class and came to all of your extra help sessions. Please, I'll do anything."

I had stood under too many umbrellas as a child when it wasn't raining. Probably because in Louisiana, folks like to honor the dead with jazz funerals. They include playing solemn hymns and walking under sun-brellas. The name, "second-line," took the place for these rituals. Mainly, the secondary guest would participate in them behind the main family members.

You can see what a, "second-line," is at the Jazz Festival in New Orleans because they break out at random times when people feel the urge to start one on the Fairgrounds. Maybe by 80 my bad luck would fade, but by then, I might be dead from a heart attack due to living in a state with such good, cheap fried food.

Professor Hynes responded to my pleas for help. "You can't just have an A for effort. It must be demonstrated. Organic Chemistry is a difficult course."

Now she sounded condescending, and I couldn't stand her arrogance. "I'm not asking for an A. This will ruin my life. You're a teacher. You're supposed to help!" My voice level definitely rose.

"It's out of my control." She responded.

I felt if I ever showed emotion, I would lose the protection I had built for myself, but now, I was about to lose it, even though it was obvious that tears wouldn't make this woman budge.

I turned to leave and smacked into a blonde girl standing in the doorway. There were at least a hundred people in the Organic Chemistry class, but I recognized her because she was unique. She sat in the back of the room near the door and always had a new hair color every month.

Besides this bizarre attribute, she stuck out in another way. She was at least ten years older than the rest of us and must have been catching up on education. At the rate I was moving, I hoped I wouldn't be finishing college that old. I wondered how long she had been present listening to my humiliation.

"I hope I'm not interrupting."

"We're finished." I turned back around to shoot Professor Hynes a cold look. "Wait, I mean, I'm finished." At least I wasn't as snotty as Jackson. My roommate would have said *she* paid the Professor's salary and demanded her grade be changed or else she would have the Professor fired.

I left the office but stood around the corner, curious to hear what Professor Hynes said to the girl. I automatically didn't like her when the Professor told her she did an outstanding job in the class.

I headed for the library and moments later, I sat at my job at the information desk, tapping my fingers, squirming in my seat as I studied my loan statements and pondered how to stay in school. I needed ten thousand dollars to replace my scholarship money. I always thought education was the one thing that couldn't be taken away from me. I thought it was priceless. Apparently, because it looked like I'd be paying for it for years.

I knew I should have chosen LSU, where the tuition was under two thousand dollars a semester. But, when the scholarship from Tulane came through, I thought I finally had an opportunity to get out of Louisiana. Students from all over the country would be attending Tulane. I had a chance to be surrounded by cultures rather than a sheltered small town. The school rank was also higher and I saw it as a way to move up in the world.

It was amazing how one class could trigger a chain of events in my life. I thought about Isaac Newton's first law of motion. "An object in motion tends to stay in motion, and an object at rest tends to stay at rest, unless the object is acted upon by an outside force." Although I had learned the concept in High School, I really didn't get to apply it until now. Real life experiments were far more beneficial than classroom lessons designed to prove or disprove a theory. Lately, my life was one big experiment in inertia.

My minimum wage library job would hardly cover the money I needed to stay in school. Last year, I had the, "freshman fifteen," but for me it was the "freshman negative fifteen." I didn't make enough money to get wasted and eat pizza after a night out with friends.

I occasionally let Jackson spoil me with her money, but I didn't want anything from anyone. Foster dad number six had said when you are given something you must pay it back. But he broke child labor laws when he took me out of school and had me work all day in his rat infested Deli. I was moved from that home right away.

The pay wasn't the only problem with my library job. The location of my desk on the third floor was more of a social club than a place to study. According to *The Princeton Review*, the third floor was ranked as one of the best pick-up places for coeds. When students asked me to help them find a book, I would tell them exactly which row to find it in. There was no way I wanted to go into the stacks and see making out between giggling girls and coercive boys.

Daddies would be happy to know their angels were joining the literary equivalent to a mile-high club in an airplane. I had never been on a plane, but watched enough movies to know the meaning of the club.

Also, the library got on my last nerve because every time I got to the exciting part of a novel or tried to do that Organic Chemistry homework, indolent students asking how to use the computers to search for a book, interrupted me. They were already set-up waiting for incompetent students, the ones who took the "I." All they had to do was type what they wanted in the blank box and press enter.

I was about to put my loan statements away, when I saw footsteps headed towards my desk, presumably from one of those slack students who must have waited until the last possible second to finish a semester project. "Let's get this over with fast." I mumbled softly. My eyes remained on my papers that I held close to my face. "We close at 4 p.m. in observance of Christ's birthday tomorrow."

"Can I look at the Physics books Professor Kenmore placed on reserve, sweetie?"

"If you call me something that doesn't rhyme with a fictional bird." I reluctantly got off my ass and slapped my papers on the desk coming face to face with Blondie from Professor Hynes class. Just the person I wanted to see. Fates way of slapping me in the face was to make me look at the girl whose academic record surpassed mine and most likely ruined the curve for me and all the students on the third floor.

I got off my seat to find the books on the reserve shelf behind my chair. I handed them to her.

"So, you're pre-med too?" She asked.

"A double major in business." I wanted to let her know that I had a heavier load than she did, and that *that* was the only reason she beat me in the class.

"No wonder you're having a tough time. You know, forty percent of pre-med majors drop it for another area of study."

"I'm not having a tough time."

"You seemed upset in Professor Hynes' office. That was you, right?"

"Since no zygote was split that I know of, yes."

"Well, I know you're *not* having a hard time in your business classes." She was right about that. Everyone knew the reputation was that the, "B," school was just that. No work and you could easily have a B. A little more effort, an A. But I didn't see where any of this was her business. No pun intended.

"You know what, I really don't want to discuss this with a stranger." I was being a real bitch, but I didn't want to stand there with this girl grilling me.

She didn't seem hurt by my rejection. "I have to go study. It doesn't come so easily to me."

Was she kidding? She was the one who got a B in one of the hardest classes.

Thirty minutes later, Blondie was back to bother me. I was reading a book about a girl who became a prostitute to pay for school. Definitely not how I wanted to turn out. My loan statements acted as my bookmarker.

"Can I trouble you for Professor Copley's reserve books now?" Not a hint of rudeness for my brushing her aside earlier.

"You finished *that* fast?"

"I only needed a few things from it." She placed the book back on the counter.

As I turned back around to hand her the new books, I caught her eyeing my desk. She pulled my loan statements from the fiction novel. In her case, the, "I," stood for *impulsive.*

"Is this a handout I was supposed to read for one of our classes?"

I knew she wasn't doing well in pre-med by being an idiot, and I defensively grabbed my papers back. "Since you're so nosy, I'm losing my scholarship money. Now I have to drop out of school. And to top it off, I will have to restart paying my loans unless I want to go into default and have my credit blown for the rest of my life."

I had reversed my position on being tight lipped with her, and I took a dramatic deep breath as if telling this stranger my problems had relinquished the anxiety I felt.

The girl just stood there smiling at me. "The street will help you save some money so you can come back. Taking a semester off isn't so bad." Her bravado made me want to slap her.

It looked like she had taken years of semesters off. My anxiety heightened with the thought of graduating ten years from now.

"What street? Do I look like a whore to you?"

"I don't know if you're a whore, but I'm not. I'm talking about Bourbon Street, sweetie. Oops. Sorry, no more fictional birds. Speaking of cartoons, I always preferred Jerry."

"Mice are pesky." I answered in response to her choice of a Hanna Barbera character over Warner Brother's Looney Tunes.

Ignoring my slight, she continued. "Anyway, the street will be dead tonight and tomorrow with everyone celebrating the birth of Christ and all." *Was she mocking my initial attempt to get rid of her?*

The only thing on Bourbon Street were restaurants and bars, mainly wild tourist clubs that we occasionally went to when we were sick of the local, smoke filled, dive bars. However, the stench in the French Quarter was worse.

Bourbon Street always reeked of a potent amalgamation of stale alcohol, vomit, and cigarettes. You had to be careful where you stepped. It smelled and looked like someone forgot to take out the trash and an animal finally tore into it, scattering it. I would say stray dogs, but mice were a more logical explanation. No wonder she preferred Jerry. I avoided Bourbon Street and preferred the solitary smell of smoke. At least you knew the potential hazardous outcome from that. There were no unknown substances.

"I'd rather not be one of those mendicants playing the guitar with the case open so people can drop money at my feet."

"We all engage in some form of begging down there, but you'll be making *a lot* more than those street artists."

"So *that's* what people call them."

The girl continued to smile at me. Was her face tattooed with a grin? I had seen what tattooed make-up looked like because Jackson's mother had permanent eye liner and lip liner. Too bad lip liner went in and out of style. I wondered if her mother would have it removed and put back on each time.

She continued with instructions. "Meet me at the streetcar stop at Canal Street at 8 p.m. on the 26th. I'll take you to a place where you can make triple bank. I guarantee it will be an exciting job. Oh, and don't be late because I have to get to my own job. I have a feeling you are responsible." Just in case I decided not to show, she scribbled her phone number and name, Beth.

I was surprised she thought I was responsible when I was fucking up in school. If she could really help me, I would have to let go of my contempt for her slaughtering me in Organic Chemistry. Life was one big competition for survival, and I had to struggle to stay on top.

Beth returned to her cubicle to study. At exactly 4 p.m., she returned the reserve books. Maybe she would be helpful. Most students returned books late and I would have to sit and wait.

I didn't receive overtime, and it would be my fault if books were missing. My biological clock for a new job was ticking.

I called after Beth as she bid, "adieu."

"You didn't get my name. It's Calina."

"I know." Her inflection told me I was silly for thinking she didn't.

Chapter 2

I left the library and headed through campus to my dorm. From nine p.m. December 24th until January 13th, students were supposed to find alternative living arrangements. The electricity would still be on, but at nine p.m. I would have to turn the lights off and pretend I wasn't there or risk being fined. Supposedly, they had resident advisors monitoring the dorm. I wondered where other students with no home went. Maybe I was the only one.

I had spent the first five years of my life in New Orleans, and I always considered it my true home before I began moving around the state as a result of foster care. The year before I turned eighteen and was kicked out of foster care, I finally made it back. A well-to-do family living on Saint Charles Avenue, the Holts, took me in. Their daughter, Annabel, had gone to Tulane and they were now empty nesters wishing they had had more children.

I didn't think anyone who grew up in New Orleans could be as big a goodie-goodie as Annabel was, but her parents sheltered her. Annabel was convinced I couldn't get into Tulane. I overheard her tell her mom that, "small town education must be horrible."

I set out to prove her wrong and then some. Annabel's parents were paying full tuition on her education. I decided I would receive a scholarship. Annabel wouldn't even say congratulations when the admission and scholarship came through. Her parents were extremely proud of me, and it felt nice to have someone in my corner for the first time in years.

Last year, I had gone to the Holts for Christmas. They gave me nice presents and spending money, even after they were no longer financially responsible for me. Soon after Christmas, Annabel began to tell vicious lies to turn her parents against me. Girls are wicked when they're jealous. Annabel got her hands on some particular shower photos, and I was no longer invited to the Holts.

It would be a lonely Christmas so I stopped at the campus convenience store for some non-perishable items. I couldn't use the appliances in the communal kitchen and risk being found and kicked out. I began my grocery shopping by placing a box of Cocoa Puffs cereal in my cart. I really needed to make an effort to eat healthier. I didn't eat that much though, having trained my stomach at an early age to miss meals.

Back in 88, I had a cult leader, Peter Paul, for a foster father. He was small time compared to Jim Jones and David Koresh. He offered rice and beans or nothing. I usually went with nothing. The beans made my stomach hurt. I am still bitter about the rice and beans because I won't eat sushi rolls. I hear they are very tasty, but whenever I go to sushi with Jackson, I stick to the sashimi.

These days, I didn't really want to spend tons of money on something so transitory, and I didn't feel the necessity to placate the angry child growling inside. I picked up some meal replacement bars. They would be healthier, with their claim of being a balanced meal substitute, but they went against my money issue because they were expensive. Next, I grabbed some microwave soups.

Mmm. Ice cream. Although the thirty-one flavors of Baskin Robbins were my favorite, they didn't carry the brand on campus. I couldn't help but pick a little container of another brand that would fit in the little mini-fridge/freezer we had in the room. I walked up to the freezer and saw my usual Breyers selection. Then, I saw that they had added a new selection of Dreyer's.

Did Breyers or Dreyer's create the other brand just to piss off whatever brand came out first? Or did the same company own them both and the second brand was created to bring in more money from a seemingly new product? I would have to look the companies up on the Internet. Screw pre-med. It was all about marketing. At least I had learned something in my business classes.

I went to the counter and unloaded my items, handing the clerk my meal plan card. "You owe fowtee dollars." The clerk announced.

"What? I thought I had money left."

"You got ten dollars."

I rifled through my wallet remembering where all the money on my card had gone. A week before, Jackson and I needed a study break and went out for a drink. Unfortunately, it was happy hour at the Last Stop, a bar ten feet from the campus property line. I thought the named suited the bar quite well because all the college students convened here before going home with that random person of the opposite sex, or same sex in some cases not as widely noticed, but when publicized caused an uproar.

I preferred quarter pitcher nights at another bar down the street, since that was more in my budget. However, The Last Stop's happy hour drinks were cheap, mass sized proportions where one drink equaled two. By the time we were finished, Jackson and I had both had six.

After we had gotten drunk, Jackson coerced me to get a pizza from BamBam's. They took the meal plan cards, and I used mine because she forgot hers. She didn't have her credit cards and was always losing them anyway. She promised to pay me back, but I guess we forgot, and I couldn't hound her since she normally paid.

I handed the clerk the only twenty in my wallet. "I guess I have to put back a few things." Shwanda must have recognized my body language when I shrunk my shoulders in defeat and the downward expression in my eyes when I turned around to put the items back.

"Tell you what. See them cameras? They ain't working so just put that ice cream back and keep them meal replacement bars.

Ice cream's on a stricter inventory check and them meal replacement bars is more healthy anyway. I seen you in here before. You nicer than the others."

I knew what she meant. She grew up in the projects of New Orleans and was most likely still there. Working at a private University predominately made up of rich kids probably wasn't a dream job come true. Not that everyone was an exact replica of each other, but the snooty kids from New York didn't make her job any easier. My own roommate demanded on more than one occasion that they order Ben and Jerry's Chunky Monkey immediately or find it from another store while a line of students stood waiting at the checkout counter. Jackson knew there was no other convenience store on campus. After all, she had her breakfast bagels flown in from New York.

I pushed the bars back towards Shwanda. "Thanks, but I don't want to get you in trouble."

She pushed them back towards me. I felt like we were playing a board game taking turns trying to beat each other to the finish line. "I can always say I took them bars. We get a certain amount of discount working here."

Her family was probably worse off than me. Not much though. "I can't let you do that."

"Take em." She shoved the meal replacement bars in my bag, and I thanked her for her generosity. Or *dishonesty*, in the University's case.

When I got back to my room, I was beat from my day of teacher pleading, boring library work, and worrying about money. Just as I was about to fall asleep on my bed, I realized I would have to find a new place to live since I wouldn't be returning for the semester. If only I could buy some time. *Well, not literally.*

I couldn't keep taking handouts from people like Shwanda who didn't have much to give. I rose from the bed and opened the classified section of the Times Picayune that I had taken from the library. Okay, I know I really stole it, but come on-it was Christmas Eve and no one would be worried about the classified section. Of course, no one would pick up the phone on Christmas Eve either and the harsh reality that I didn't have a resume that would warrant any more than minimum wage made me sink further into my bad mood.

I turned on the computer and scoured the school's website and found every opportunity was similar to the desk job I already had. I pulled out Beth's phone number from my bag and stared at the little smiley face she drew under her name. I was curious about her. Chipper, older college students weren't the norm. Especially here. I was interested in the place where she said I could make triple bank.

I looked at the clock. In an hour, I would have to turn out the lights and pretend no one was home. I finally got my own room for a little while, and I had to pretend that I didn't exist. In foster care, I never had my own space. I moved from one bad home to the next. I was always placed in homes with too many children. The foster parents just wanted money from the state.

There was one other time in the early days of foster care that I had my own room, but it was only because one child said I hit them which was the farthest thing from the truth. I was locked in a room for a few days with only a board game, *Sorry*. The mother said I couldn't come out until I learned that word. But I wouldn't back down on my declaration that I hadn't made a mistake.

I played that board game and had to be two players at the same time. When she heard me, she yelled at me for talking to myself when I spoke for the other player. I couldn't win. In fiction or non. I thanked Milton Bradley for allowing me to develop an imagination that would take me farther in life than aspiring to be a waitress at Waffle House. No offense to my friend Darlene back in Bogalusa.

My time at the Holt's home gave me a taste of having a room all to myself, but then I jumped right back into a dysfunctional situation in college. Jackson and I were randomly selected roommates. The situation was like *Sorry*. *At first.* She was too cool for me, until I helped her with a computer class towards the end of our first semester. She gained a new respect for me. Or, maybe she just realized that I was useful.

However, we became good friends, and I started to party with her. Come to think of it, Jackson was the trigger for my life turning into a Newton law, not Professor Hynes. I knew I was at school to study and do well so I could find a job when I got out of college or get into medical school, but party animal Jackson began to drag me down with her. She had a way of making me feel bad if I didn't comply. I was through with that. Look where it had gotten me. Grades and doing well in school were of no consequence to her. With all of her money and connections, she was guaranteed success in whatever she decided.

Jackson's belongings littered all over the floor only reminded me the room would never be solely mine. You had to win some lottery to get your own room on our campus. I hadn't struck housing gold.

We decided to live together again sophomore year after becoming closer freshman year, but also because Jackson's parents wouldn't allow her to live off campus with her other friends. They knew their daughter would throw parties every night. This way, she threw them at their bar and had some supervision.

They say living with good friends isn't a good idea, cause afterwards you aren't so close anymore. Whoever, "they," are, "they," were correct. Maybe we needed some distance and my leave of absence from school would be a good thing. After college, I wanted to live alone so I wouldn't have to put up with a messy roommate and being sent to home base because I was kicked off the board. I didn't see my name being synonymous with stability anytime soon.

For someone raised in opulence, Jackson was a slob. Her clothes littered the floor. It was beyond me how someone could treat designer clothes with such indifference. She was probably used to other people picking up after her. I felt like her maid, but I did have a knack for catching dust before it hit the floor.

I hung her clothes in her closet, but then slipped into a Viviane Westwood dress. Maybe I would wear it while she was gone. The dress looked better on me because Jackson's gluttony for booze and late night treats had taken their toll. Her mother had already yelled at her for being the heftiest socialite daughter of the year, according to the new *Teen People* Magazine. She blamed it on the freshman fifteen, but was more annoyed when they gave Chelsea Clinton and her relationship with her mom a full eight-pages and only gave Jackson a quarter of a page for the Valentino she wore to the sorority formal.

After hanging up her clothes, I found her ashtray shoved in her open dresser drawer. Gross. I threw the cigarettes and the ashtray in the trash. Maybe if she had to scrounge for another one, she would quit smoking. Yeah, right. For Jackson, smoking was something that she could regulate and *not* her parents. It's kind of like girls with eating disorders that know they're not fat, but food is something in their lives they have control over.

Cigarettes also functioned as a symbol of stress relief. I occasionally had one, but I wasn't a chain smoker like Jackson. The tobacco made my naturally wired body more riled up. What was wrong with us? We all knew smoking was hazardous to our health, yet we kept on lighting up.

When I finished cleaning, I remembered that Jackson left me a present for Christmas. I would open it now to make my current circumstances less depressing. I lifted her mattress to find the present she said she left. I found a tiny, blue box from some store named after a Tiffany chick. Maybe this was what the girls meant when they were talking about their bracelets and Tiffany. She certainly didn't want jewelry stolen, so it was smart of her to hide it.

I grew excited at the notion that the other girls wouldn't have to stop talking about expensive things when I came around. Jackson was a culprit too, until she got to know me. Just because I didn't carry a Prada handbag or a Kate Spade bag, some of her friends turned their noses up. Literally. If I took a picture of them, it would look like they were staring up at a plane in the sky.

Maybe it was because I had a neutral accent and they hated that I didn't sound so nasally like they did. Or maybe it was because when they saw me without parents on parents' weekend, they knew. Knew that I didn't belong to the wealthy, upper crust families that they did, but was a gypsy.

When I entered school, I thought I had had a screwed up life, but many of the rich kids had just as many, if not more issues than me. The truth was, their families were more screwed up than mine, or my lack of one. The current hot song played at the Last Stop was P.Diddy's, "Mo Money Mo problems." Ain't that the truth.

Jackson wanted me to be in their sorority, but they didn't pick me to be a member. Sometimes, I thought she hung out with me more than her, "sisters," to rebel against them, but it was nice that she stuck by me and showed them that she wasn't going to stop hanging out with me.

There was a note on top of the Tiffany box. 'Merry Christmas, Calina. Something to help you chill out since exams are over.' A bracelet wasn't a chill out present. I opened the top lid.

Inside, I stared at a Ziploc baggie filled with marijuana. Great, something that wouldn't last. And how dare she tell me I needed to chill out! Now, I really needed some air, but I was afraid to leave the room if I didn't absolutely have to. The person patrolling could be near, waiting to check the rooms.

I went for the pipe hidden in Jackson's closet. I only smoked with Jackson a handful of times because she provided it. I hated taking handouts from her, but this was the *one* thing I would always take without worry about paying it back. There was some unwritten rule that it didn't matter. Some people just never want to do drugs alone. She smoked when I wasn't around, as well. Research showed it wasn't good for people below twenty. Yet, I lit up and inhaled.

If President Clinton did it and was successful, then I could too. I loved pot. As soon as I inhaled, my body relaxed. My internal dialogue would sometimes bother me, but I usually made myself laugh.

I headed for the radio and blasted it. Woops. I quickly turned it off. Wasn't I supposed to be quiet for some reason? Oh yeah, a resident advisor was patrolling the premises at nine p.m. But I wanted to dance. Hmm, maybe I'd put on the TV or watch a movie. I went for the TV. But wait, I couldn't turn the volume up for some reason, so I'd have to struggle to hear. What was that reason again? Oh yeah, the dorm nerd. *Shit.* I got stoned fast.

My hunger kicked in. The ice cream would have been great right about now. I had no choice but soup and heated it. As I took it out of the microwave, I heard the door next to my room slam shut. Was it already 9 p.m.? I put the soup down fast and stifled a scream as it tipped over the Tupperware and burned me. I dumped Jackson's huge laundry basket on her bed all over the floor as a distraction tactic and ran to the closet to hide.

Keys turned in my door, and it flew open. I could feel eyes scouring the room, and I held my breath. They *did* have people monitoring the place. What was the point? If someone was babysitting, why couldn't we be here? What a great Christmas Eve, hiding out in a closet, drugs for a present, and soggy soup for dinner. Although an Atheist by day, I was happy I was Jewish by birth.

"Jackson? Calina? Anyone home?"

Did it look like I still occupied the room? Surely cologne and perfume still lingered, suggesting that people had *recently* left? *Uh-oh.* What about the pot smell? I could see through a crack in the middle of the double doors of the closet that two feet stood close. I began to sweat.

Had the, "y," of yes accidentally slipped from my mouth before I realized it wasn't one of our friend's voices? No, that was something Jackson would have done. Wow, I was turning into her. I was even developing a New York accent pronouncing the Last Stop the Last Stooop and the phone the fon. That's not very easy when you've lived in multiple po-dunk towns your whole life. *Oh god, it's me Calina. Please don't let him find me. I'll forget about the atheist bullshit. I promise. I know you're really there. You have to be.*

I could see Dorm Nerd walk over to our desks. He appeared to be studying our photographs. He wouldn't know who was who in the pictures because we had a table between our desks with pictures of both of us scattered around. We used to have those block letters that look like they're cut out of the newspaper or a magazine to display our names. We both took them down because we knew who was who and our friends knew who was who. Name displays were also a very freshman thing to do. Although, Jackson was probably scared that someone would confuse our identities. The closets *were* labeled. No doubt Jackson's insistance.

What the hell was I thinking about again? Oh yeah, Dorm Nerd looking at the pictures. I contemplated the situation and thought I was going to laugh. I was hiding out in a closet from, I assumed, some poor pimply guy. The only reason I contained my giggles was because I had no place to live. That was enough to scare me straight.

Dorm Nerd turned away from the closet and fixated on the pile of clothes I had dumped on the floor. The diversionary tactic worked. "What a rich slob." He said as he began to rummage through the pile. He picked up a piece of my lingerie. *Eww.*

Little did he know, a few years later, there would be a reality show created by the guy I showered with in the freshman dorms where they videotaped people sneaking around and going through things in other peoples' dorm rooms. He had some kind of voyeur problem.

His friends were the ones that gave Annabel the evidence that I was a, "bad girl." Annabel was in the prim and proper sorority, but I heard they were closet sluts. My, "bad girl," act was only a shower in the guys' bathroom, and I was still dressed in a bra and panties.

I thought of Annabel one more time in my life in June of 2000, when I watched a season three episode of *Sex in The City* called, "Attack of The Five-Foot-Ten Woman." Samantha brings a woman, Jenna who went to Tulane and is dressed like a debutante to an event to provide Carrie with information about her ex-boyfriend's new wife, Natasha.

Jenna reports that at Tulane, Freshman year, Natasha once showered with a guy in a community bathroom. Carrie, a *sex* columnist, looks at her like, "so, what's the big deal?" The only other information Jenna can provide is that Natasha gained weight Sophomore year.

Making Natasha sound, "bad," doesn't make Carrie feel any better about herself. It only makes her feel worse. I doubted Annabel had the insight to eventually feel worse by gossiping about my innocuous incident. And, as evidenced by *Sex and The City*, multiple coeds must have been partaking in shower scenes.

Dorm Nerd's footsteps headed back towards the closet. *Oh shit.* God obviously *wasn't* listening. Atheism was back on. He turned again and headed over to my CD rack. I saw through one eye that he pulled out my brand new Madonna CD. *But god, that wasn't your intervention. It was his taste in music. Next time, I promise I'll give up the Atheism. Next time.*

Dorm Nerd left with my Madonna CD still in his hands! Jesus, if I had known a Madonna CD would get him out of there, I would have left them around the room like cheese for pesky mice.

I left the closet and returned to the microwave to reheat the quarter of the soup still left in the Tupperware. Dorm Nerd would be dancing to Madonna's, "Ray of Light," now. I was safe.

Chapter 3

All day on the 25th, I had a hide and read party. My interest in books and learning took hold at age eight, when I was in a home with two drunks. They used to guzzle beer and argue by the TV. Drunk Bob used to come looking to harass me, but he could never find me.

I was having hide and read parties in the closet with a flashlight. From the *Sweet Valley High* series, I learned about drunk driving, rape, divorce, dating and sex. I could read fast and read books that were above my age level. When Drunk Ann would see them, she would explain to me that I had to read books for my own age. She didn't get the concept of advancement.

On the 25th, I called the one lady who always believed in my future potential, to wish her a Merry Christmas. Ella Ferguson never blamed me for the deception. I was only eleven and following orders from a foster mother, Irene. No one should be taking in foster kids when they have seven people on a twenty-four-thousand-dollar budget.

Irene told me I must do what she said in order to stay in the family. I didn't really care, but didn't have much of a choice when she told me to just keep repeating, "what?" at the pediatrician's office.

She told him, "She just lost her hearing doctor. No accidents or nothin."

Irene explained on the way home that we needed some extra money, and if they thought I had a disability, they would send help to the house for me, but more importantly, extra *money*.

"Can I have extra books for playing the role? Actors get paid you know."

Irene did give me the books, but her charade didn't go as planned. There was no money for in home care, and they sent me away to a home for the deaf and blind. Ella was in charge of me.

Ella taught me sign language, and I watched her help the kids who really *did* have disabilities. I grew fond of her. I wanted to help the other kids too and make Ella proud of me. I began to appreciate education and how lucky I was to actually have my hearing.

Ella suspected I might have regained my hearing and did some tests on me. After confessing everything, I told her I didn't want to leave. The home was better than any foster care house I had ever lived. She tried to adopt me, but there was too much controversy over Irene's lie that Ella's job was threatened. People also didn't look favorably on biracial adoptions back then. She said it wasn't my fault, and she could talk to me on the phone.

On the 26th, I woke late with a crick in my neck from my second night of sleeping in the closet. Dorm Nerd was on to me. I heard him walking around outside and this time, I hid in the bathroom stall. I wanted to go to the store and buy chloroform to knock him out if he bothered me, but somehow I knew I didn't need a criminal offense added to my poverty status. *Hmm.* At least in jail I would have a permanent bed.

I hadn't left my room in two days and was beginning to go all Jack Nicholson in *The Shining.* Although, I thought it was worse to be confined in a small space than a giant hotel. It would be nice to have more light because the natural light seeping in through the closed blinds wasn't enough while I was kickin' it in the closet. I wondered why Dorm Nerd didn't just open the blinds? That would save him the energy of opening the door to see if anyone was home.

I gave Beth a call to find out what I should wear that evening. "Calina, I'm so glad you called. I can't wait to see you." She told me to wear jeans and a tank top, but if I had black shorts and sneakers to bring them to change into. They would provide me with a crop top. I needed a job badly, but I didn't want to parade around in a shirt that showed an orifice, no matter how small it was. Skimpy clothing just reminded me of women in my past and the men who used to criticize them and say, "the less clothes the mo hos."

After dressing later that evening, I slowly opened the door and peered out. I didn't see anyone, but I did see a piece of silver tape connecting my door to its socket. The building administrators were so lame. Or was it Dorm Nerd's idea? They thought they could catch people breaking the rules with tape? I shut the door and went to find our stash of silver duct tape from when we had a hurricane threat in August.

Southerners and East Coasters learn that putting duct tape on the windows helps to protect the glass from spraying every which way if the hurricane winds did shatter it. I figured high winds would destroy the place regardless of the sticky stuff.

Hell, New Orleans is supposed to be under water in 50 years. Not only is it 8-11 feet below sea level, eighty percent of all wetland loss in the United States occurs in Louisiana and we lose approximately 16,000 acres a year.

Outside, I cut a piece of tape off the roll and turned around to place a new piece on the door. I thought I was smooth, but really, it was just my natural instinct for survival. I had a whole head filled with tactics of hiding and escaping.

I waited on St. Charles Avenue by Walnut Street for the red streetcar with green trim. In New Orleans, it was Christmas all year. I turned around and faced Audubon Park, staring at the mansions on Walnut Street. Turning thirty degrees, I faced The ParkView Guesthouse situated on the street corner. I wished I could stay there tonight.

I turned back around and faced the gated mansions across the street where 24-hour security guards sat in a little booth. One day, I wanted to live shielded from the outside world on a gated street. Instead of, "Beware of Dog," a sign would welcome, "No

Threat of Violence." The noisy streetcar screeched down the tracks.

Twenty-minutes later, I exited on Canal Street and waited for Beth who got off on the next streetcar. She informed me that on Bourbon Street her name was Celexa. "Some customers can be crazy stalkers, so it's best to pretend you have two lives."

The street always sounded like a suitcase being noisily wheeled by someone in an airport, the click clicking of the wheels as they roll against the tile floor like the street dancers with their silver painted bodies tapping away for tips from passersby. We weaved in and out trying to avoid them, as well as the street musicians strumming their guitars.

Drunks and sobers of all colors, ages, and sizes came at us all at once, staring up at partiers dangling beads off of the wrought iron balconies instead of looking straight ahead to watch where they were going. I hated large groups of people congregated in tight spaces. How would I work down here?

A petite blonde girl no more than eighteen nodded at us. Celexa informed me the girl worked on the street and soon, I too would be able to see the great camaraderie that existed between the service industry workers and recognize who was in our world by a simple glance. It was in the eyes and the gait. The gait, fast paced, not ogling like a tourist, determined to reach our destination quickly and efficiently without being propositioned to flash for Mardi Gras beads at all times of the year. The eyes, as if to say, "what are we doing here on one of the vilest, most disgusting, and overall crazy streets in the good old US of A," yet knowing it was all about the money.

"Praise Jesus. Praise Jesus. Take sin out of your life, and put Jesus back in." I looked up to see a few people standing around a fifteen foot cross handing out pamphlets on saving yourself from the evils in the world. I was sure drugs and alcohol were high on that list. One of the men grabbed Celexa's arm. "You. You are a tempter of men. A facilitator of sin. God hates sin. Jesus is your answer."

"Fuck off." Celexa pulled her arm free and shoved the man. I saw her smile fade for the first time. "Those Bible people are freaks. Make sure you stay away from them."

She didn't have to worry. I thought religion was devotion run amok. I dropped it after Peter Paul, the one who pushed the rice and beans, had me waking up at all hours to pray. When social services checked on me, he told them I had a lot of energy and wanted to play at all hours of the night. Despite my weight loss and glazed eyes from sleep deprivation, the social worker told me I needed to listen to my poppa better. Now, on Bourbon Street, I was witnessing the big city freaks who had probably trained that sorry excuse for a, "Poppa."

When Celexa announced that we had arrived at our destination, I saw a girl on stage dancing with leis around her neck, a veil on the top of her head, one friend making a blow-up doll gyrate with her, another feeding her shots and the last holding an inflatable penis near her face. I assumed the girl was a bride to be and was living it up for her last days of bachelorettedom.

"It's another night of debauchery on Bourbon Street."

"One you can benefit from." Celexa responded as we stopped in front of a huge neon sign that read, "Black Sevens."

"They wanted a name with the same abbreviation as Bourbon Street." She told me.

"Sounds more like a card game to me."

I had never been to this club because I normally avoided cheesy tourist clubs and because we just went to Jackson's parent's club when we hit the French quarter scene. I had to be really drunk to deal with tourist clubs. It could be fun to flirt with tourists because you didn't have to run into them again, as opposed to guys at school. However, tourists were annoying because they assumed you were another tourist. My tone would convey my annoyance when I told them I liked to be challenged by pick up lines. Then, a nasty confrontation would ensue with the tourist turning defensive.

K.C. and The Sunshine Band blared through the large speakers by the stage. *That's The Way I Like it.* Celexa waved to the man in the DJ booth. "That's DJ Ray-Ray. He plays every decade here, from the 70's on. He overplays this song. You'll also get sick of hearing Lynyrd Skynrd's *Sweet Home Alabama*, Abba's *Dancing Queen*, Wild Cherry's *Play That Funky Music*. You get the point. He was a teenager back then. It reminds him of his glory days when he wore platforms, big frilly shirts with those dangling collars and snorted coke so he could dance all night."

"I'm a nineties teen. Nirvana. Stone Temple Pilots. We're all angst ridden."

"That's no fun. I was an eighties teen. Blow and cheesy ballads."

Celexa stopped behind a man who examined a register receipt. He turned and greeted her with a long hug, eyeing me curiously. He must have been gorgeous in his twenties. His blue eyes still sparkled, but with the late hours he worked in the club and no time to exercise, his slight beer belly protruding, streaks of gray hair and slight wrinkles on his tan skin definitely aided his aging process. Celexa told me later he was only thirty-six.

"What up girl? How's work treating you?"

"Depends which one. Number one is the same old bullshit. Part performance art, part male manipulation. Number two is....well, you know. Here's the new girl for you. She needs the money." Then she whispered, "She's a smart one, but she's about to loose her scholarship. Been on the minimum wage scale."

"Standing right here." I said.

The man ignored my comment and instructed me to turn around. I looked at him oddly, but did as I was told and twirled around.

"Her butt don't look like it."

"I see you like to shoot your mouth off. How does my chest look?"

"You got cojones, girl. I'm gonna like you. Name's Will Toscano."

Will was a, "Yat," or middle class New Orleanian who spoke with an accent resembling Brooklynese mixed with a southern drawl. He glared at me, intimidating me. I always knew I was smarter than the people around me, but now I was in a different league. I didn't know the surroundings, which put me at a disadvantage. Growing up, every situation was different, but there was always a commonality about how things worked in foster care.

"You from the Bayou?" He laughed.

"No. Dad was New Orleans heat killed in the line of duty when I was five. Mom died a year later, and I went into foster care. Lived all over Louisiana since, but I prefer N'awlins."

"Oh wow. How old are ya?"

"19."

"Here's the deal. You can start tonight because a girl didn't show. This business is like that. Frequent turnaround. We don't care if the girls come and go cause we always got another one waitin."

I didn't care how the business ran. I just needed a well-paid job. "What exactly is the position?"

"See that girl?" He pointed to a girl wearing a green crop top that said Black Sevens, black shorts, and ugly black sneakers. She was holding a tray of test tubes.

I nodded. Back to High School science experiments. Next thing I knew someone would come out walking around with Bunsen Burners. Was Isaac Newton sending me a sign? I could *not* see this place answering my money woes.

"You're a tooter girl. Also known as a, "shot girl." You carry forty test tubes of booze around the club. You also act as a cocktail waitress and get customers regular drinks." He continued to explain I would get five bucks from the club for each tray I sold, plus tips from customers. His voice drifted into the background like extraneous television dialogue. My thoughts were in the forefront. I had never had a job where the money was based on performance.

My former jobs consisted of clerk in a grocery store, clerk in a clothing store with no commission, and babysitting at a flat rate of $2.50 an hour. I never wanted to be a waitress because I was afraid of getting stuck.

I figured Celexa was bringing me down to the Street to be a waitress, but *not* an alcohol pusher. I could see Mother's Against Drunk Driving coming after me accusing me of seducing their sons into buying the final shot they drank before their untimely accidents.

Will was still babbling. Something about the liquor content in each shot. He must really be into his job. "This ain't a coffee shop but something's always brewing." He laughed at his attempt to crack a joke. It was a good thing Celexa hadn't brought me to a coffee shop because with my current anxiety levels, Folgers would be too much coffee in my cup.

She read the apprehension behind my scowling expression. "It's like acting, Cal." Suddenly, we were on a nickname basis.

"You just shimmy around, pretend you're a model or something and talk to them. Act like what they say is the most important thing you've ever heard, and they'll give you nice tips."

I wondered if Bourbon Street was intentionally abbreviated BS as in the art of *bullshit*. But I wasn't an actress. I didn't pretend to like things. Although, I did watch a lot of TV in order to imitate accents to avoid sounding like a southern redneck.

I decided I wanted to be an actress at age nine, but the dream was shattered. Along with reading a ton of books as I grew up, I watched a lot of television shoes and movies because there weren't many people around me to have intellectual conversations with, let alone civil ones. I was in the movie *Steel Magnolias*. It was filmed in the town I was living in at the time, Natchitoches, and I was discovered at the local diner. I was only an extra in the wedding reception scene, but I had a great time on the dance floor. Two years later, I was still with the same family and was into local theatre productions.

When I heard there was a casting call in New Orleans for the film *JFK,* I desperately wanted to go. In those two years I had grown quite nicely, not needing braces like most other children my age. However, Mother Nature hadn't been kind to the biological children of the family. My foster parents knew their girls were jealous of me and told me I couldn't go. The excuse was that Hollywood was for people who were infected by the devil.

Everyone thinks *Cinderella* is a fairytale, but I identified with her when I found out my foster parents took their real daughters to the casting call. Maybe the fairytale part isn't true, but Act I and II were reality.

I watched *Steel Magnolias* over and over again. I realized why fate had made me collide with the film. I had to become like Sally Field's character. When she tells her friends that, "men are supposed to be made of steel or something," regarding her being the only one who could sit with her daughter as the plug was pulled, I knew how I would have to be in life to deal with families that I didn't belong to. I would be a brick wall no one could break down. I didn't want to get emotionally attached.

"Good luck, Calina." Celexa turned to leave and brought me back to the reality that I was now about to work in a Bourbon Street nightclub. She would return to pick me up at the end of my shift. I wondered where she worked.

Will opened the door to the upstairs office and told me to go talk to Randy. Upstairs, I found a fat man sitting behind a desk. He had an ugly, greasy rat-tail for hair towards the end of his bald head. Apparently, he missed the fact that it was the late 90's, and mullets were out. When he stood up, he had the largest ass protruding from his backside, and I decided I would secretly call him Round Randy.

"When you bring me the money, make sure the bills face the same direction." *Nice introduction.* He opened his wallet and pulled out a few hundreds to demonstrate how Ben Franklin's face had to point in the same direction. How anal. Although, the practice probably helped when they had to send the bills to the bank. Why did he have to tempt me with Franklins? I wanted to reach out and grab them, even if some turned out to be Hamiltons. I hoped this place would bring me many of each denomination.

He handed me a crop top. "Put that on."

"Bathroom?"

"You can change in here."

What a creep. He would learn he couldn't mess with me.

"Like I said, bathroom."

"Down the hall to the left."

I found the bathroom and slammed the door shut. When I was all dressed with my C cups crammed into the tight top, I opened the door and saw him removing a tray from a locked freezer. It was colorful. Green, pink, brown, blue, and white with gold speckles.

"You know what they are?" He asked me with his screechy voice.

"I'll learn."

"Now. You don't want to look like a dumb ass with the customers. Apple Pucker, Sex on the Beach, Jagermeister, Kamikaze, and Goldschlager."

"Got it." *Like drunk people would know the difference.* At least it was easier than Organic Chemistry.

Round Randy handed me a name pin. "You can choose a fake name to go on it if you want." I wondered if this is where Beth had become Celexa. Maybe I should have concocted a fake name too, but I thought there was something to be said for being real when everyone else around me always consciously strove to be something or someone they were not.

I figured it was the college age group. People finding themselves. But I knew from TV that New Orleans was no Los Angeles. The people surrounding me were not all actors. Most already knew what roles they were playing in life and just wanted to pretend for a little while.

I picked up the heavy tray and took a whiff of the shots. They smelled like a mixture of alcohol and fruit. I doubted they contained any nutritional value. I started back down the narrow, ornamental, wrought iron spiral staircase that seemed awkward for maneuvering with a tray of shots. If only I hadn't thought it, because I slipped on a wet step, and the tray went flying to the floor below, all forty test tubes crashing, spewing colored liquid everywhere like a grand finale of fireworks on The Fourth of July. I landed on my ample sized butt, hoping it would cushion me from a big contusion.

"What happened down there?" I heard Round Randy scream from above. I wished I had lost my scholarship from law school. At least then I would have learned how to sue for workers' compensation.

Round Randy hovered above me at the top of the steps. "Don't be so clumsy." He snapped. "You do that again and you'll owe me eighty bucks. Go get a bar back to clean up the mess you made." I grabbed a bar towel to wipe the slippery steps and noticed my hands were shaking from the excitement. I didn't like screwing up, and Round Randy made me nervous.

The alcohol was a very minute amount. It wasn't like this was a fertility lab, and I dropped all the promises of babies. I could imagine the look of horror on all those hopeful infertile couples' faces when they heard their only hope lay splattered, lying cold on the floor. They would have to hope they could adopt a newborn otherwise they might have to adopt some younger foster kid they would resent because it didn't come from them, but had already lived for five years tainted by someone else. *Yes, I have some issues.*

A large, round bellied man entered the room and asked, "You do this?" I shook my head yes and added a, "sorry." I didn't want too many enemies before I even made friends. He held out his hand and introduced himself. "Name's Eduardo, but people call me Taco." I guessed it was because of his weight. He probably ate too much of the Mexican delight. I would later find out he was forty and from Columbia, South America. He took out his wallet and showed me a credit card reading, 'Taco Burrito Empanadas.' "Will got it for me as a joke."

I smiled and offered to help clean up the disaster of wet and plastic I caused, but he told me he was used to cleaning up other peoples' mess. Not only from bartending. We had something in common. He gave me a pep talk after we finished cleaning.

"Just relax and have fun. Let me know if anyone bothers you."

I nodded and stepped out onto the club floor and suddenly felt like a teenage virgin not sure if she should go through with having sex. As I walked around the club, the voices took control of me like I imagined they did for schizophrenics. They were not comforting, but certainly encouraging.

From a big fat man: "Hey babe. Hotel Bourbon. Room 202. Why don't you swing by after work?" *Yikes*, sums that up. On to my next customer.

Even from a female: "You're hot. I'll take a vodka tonic please." That was a first for me. No one admitted to homosexuality in small towns. I told myself to smile more. After all, it was for the tips.

From a young kid, "You're cute darlin, can I buy *you* a shot?" *Wait*, he didn't even look old enough to be in the club and probably wasn't. The drinking age in New Orleans was 18 until it was raised to 21 in 1996 when the Federal government threatened to stop funding for highway projects. It didn't do anything to keep people under 21 from drinking. They could still go to the drive up daiquiri shop and get someone older to buy one for them.

The year before I came to Tulane, in 1996, the school declared residence hall rooms as private residences and under Louisiana law you *can* drink in private residences. The bars nearby didn't enjoy being raided by the police when the University made it okay. Too bad my current dorm room wasn't considered enough of a private residence so I could stay there during the holiday without someone up my ass. I guess alcohol superseded homelessness.

Another waitress approached me. "Hi, I'm Darla. You must be Calina."

"Hi, I'm the new girl. Go ahead and stare. Get the gossip over." I had the line down. Moving from one foster home to the next, I also went to many different schools. By the second one, I had my fellow peers' behavior down.

Darla was awfully perky. And awfully beautiful with jet-black hair and blue eyes that matched the food coloring in the Kamikaze.

"You know, if you do a body shot, they'll tip you more."
She told me.

"A what?"

"Just put the test tube inside your cleavage like this." Darla
demonstrated by placing the test tube in between her breasts and
telling a guy with multiple piercing around his nose, chin, and
eyebrows to take the shot from there. He lowered his head and
lifted the shot with his mouth, tilting his head back to swallow.
His friends did one too. I cringed as they put their drooling mouths
up to her cleavage. Hopefully, none of his piercings had open
wounds.

After they walked away, Darla held up the three five dollar
bills. "See, they tip more when you let them get closer."

Thanks for stating the obvious, I thought. I wasn't too big
on the idea of having some drunken stranger accidentally slobber
on me or pass on some infection. Besides, I was ticklish in the
middle of my breasts. I might accidentally jump and the liquid
would go up their noses.

"What about bartending here? I bet they make a lot?"

"Good luck. I've been here two years and still haven't
moved up. The invisible ladder. It's really hard. Unless you go all
Hollywood, and give in to the manager's couch."

"I've always wondered if the casting couch thing was true."

"Well, I'm from Los Angeles and I can tell you yes, but not all the time. There are people with talent that people recognize."

"I've always wanted to go to L.A."

"I'll bring you home sometime. Although, I don't go too often." My spirits rose. A real connection to L.A. I felt like a kid who gets a lollipop at a bank. I thought doctors' offices should give better rewards for kids than stickers. They were more difficult to visit than banks. Then again, in my case, the bank proved more difficult to visit.

Darla left and I continued to walk around. The club began to fill towards what I thought looked and felt like maximum capacity, but they never stopped allowing customers to enter. I had to lift the tray above my head to walk inside near the stage. I couldn't breathe and rested the tray on the side of the bar. Someone asked me for some shots and I complied. As they walked away, a female bartender with the nametag, "Kitty," yelled at me. "Hey new waitress! You aren't allowed to sell shots in my territory. Off the bar unless you're ordering drinks!"

What a bitch, I thought. At least I wasn't named after a Pussy.

Back at the courtyard bar, I asked Taco, "Is Kitty always so mean?"

"Ah, just to new girls. Gotta prove yourself. Hang in there. Go take a cigarette break." He handed me a cancer stick from behind his ear, and I figured why not? The place screamed bad habits, and I needed a crutch right now.

I laid my tray down and rounded the corner to go behind the bar. I heard giggling and saw Will patting a bartender on her ass. Then they kissed. He turned to me and introduced his girlfriend, Jessica, who was no more than twenty. I waved hi as I blew a smoke ring from my mouth, images of foster mother Ann before my face. That's why I normally didn't smoke. I think smoke ring flashbacks must be scarier than acid trips.

When I resumed selling, I stopped at an empty table in the middle of the courtyard area of the bar careful not to infringe on any bartender's territory. I stood next to a flaming fire. Suddenly, two men tried to put their arms through it like little kids waving their fingers through a candle flame to see if it will turn their fingers black. It's amazing how alcohol can skew judgment. Will ran up and pulled them away just in time.

The taller of the two men protested.

"I'll throw you out if you try that shit again." Will yelled.

"We thought it was a mirage man."

I felt compelled to speak. "This isn't Vegas. We're not in the desert."

Will laughed. The tall man muttered something incoherent and walked off. *What fucking idiots,* I thought.

Will looked at me. He had been following me around the club. I figured he was waiting to see if I'd fuck up.

"You got a nice ass you know."

"Excuse me?" I wanted to deck him, but held back. I needed the job. At least he hadn't grabbed it like a drunk old man.

"I'm just saying, you'll do well here." He had an odd way of saying it. "If you get fat though, we send you over to Club Decline. They think they have a good name for an after hours club, but they're morons. There's no such thing as an after hours club in New Orleans." He smiled, and I realized he was trying to make me relax in his own way. At least I would have one friend in upper management since Round Randy didn't seem too friendly.

"You know Cal, every week we have incentives for you girls. Whoever sells the most gets a bonus of 200 bucks." He must like me because he was already using my nickname like Beth had.

The pressure was on. I had to be that number one salesgirl. I would have to do those body shots Darla showed me. I thrived on challenges. But, nearing 3 a.m. I headed to the managers' office to check out. I wanted to quit. I was exhausted. Carrying that shot tray all night was heavy. I had never had such a physical job before, except for when Peter Paul made me practice shooting a 44 Magnum in case our farmhouse was ever raided by the feds.

I turned the doorknob and when it wouldn't budge, I noticed that there was a doorbell. Every other time I needed a new tray throughout the night, a manager happened to be near the door to hold it open for me. It was probably a good idea for them to keep security tight since all the cash from the shot sales resided there. And, who knew what drunken partier would head upstairs and cause some kind of trouble like those men who had tried to throw limbs into the fire.

I rang the bell just as Anita Ward's *Ring My Bell* began to play. *Hmm. Coincidence?* Or was DJ Ray-Ray watching me? Customers had been watching me all night, and video cameras were scattered all around the club. *Was big brother watching?*

The door buzzed and indicated I could now turn the knob and enter. I walked upstairs where Will sat at the manager's desk. "I don't recognize you."

"I met you through Celexa." *Was this guy on drugs?*

"No, I mean you did really well out there."

Oh. I relaxed and began to count my money. I had made two hundred bucks since 9 p.m.! I couldn't quit now. Bill after bill raised my adrenaline. Thirty-three an hour as opposed to six bucks from the library would make me more money than the combination of all my past jobs net income. The other perk was that Uncle Sam and the institution weren't going to take any of it away from me!

"You're a bar maven."

Only, I felt like a hustler. A hustler that smiles all the way to the bank.

"Welcome to Black Sevens."

Chapter 4

I sat at the bar, and Will ordered me a free drink. Alcohol was a perk to working in a bar, albeit, not a healthy one. A night of serving drinks made me yearn for alcohol. At four a.m., Celexa arrived as promised. I appreciated the fact that she didn't just leave me on Bourbon Street all alone. Not that I couldn't take on all the freaks. I was just too tired to deal.

We passed a walk-up daiquiri bar, and I was tempted to have one. Celexa told me she liked to chill after work and have a drink at another bar, but she was too tired tonight.

The four a.m. crowd hadn't mellowed out that much on Bourbon Street. A bunch of wasted guys turned to us and asked us if we wanted beads. *No, we live here*, we laughed. See the bar shirt? I pointed at the name of the club on my chest. The fascination with cheap, plastic, colored beads always struck me as odd, but even I got into the sport of seeing how many I could catch from the parades that marched through the city during Mardi Gras.

We walked past Dick's Palace, and I wondered if the illuminated mechanical legs that opened and closed in the window were ever turned off. They must be tired of spreading. At least the strip club didn't make a real girl do that. Well, in public at least.

"I dance there." Celexa pointed at the strip club, and I thought of the giant cross we had seen earlier in the night. I now understood why the Bible preacher targeted her. He knew. Yet I didn't. I would have to learn that Bourbon Street was full of subtext.

I followed Celexa across the street and through the doors of the hotel Royal Senesta where she nodded at a man in a uniform. "That's Kurt. You'll be seeing a lot of him." We headed down some steps to an underground call station for cabs where she pushed a button on the wall. The streetcars stopped running at one a.m.

My initial bias towards Beth for doing well in Organic Chemistry forgotten, I wanted to make conversation on our ride home. I asked her if she would be traveling at all during the rest of the holiday.

"My parents are in Greece. They didn't ask me to join them. I was young like you once. Rebellious though. Dropped out of school by choice. I'm trying to finish now. You live on campus?" She asked as we drove through the Garden District and entered Uptown.

I nodded yes. *Shit.* I bet anal Dorm Nerd with no life would be waiting for me to sneak back into the dorm.

As we began to ride past Audubon Park, Beth announced her stop had arrived. "If you need anything kiddo, don't be afraid to call me. Oh, and we're having a huge New Year's Party at my house so please come. I live right over there in that blue house."

She pointed to one of the mansions on Walnut Street, perpendicular to St. Charles. My mouth dropped and I quickly closed it to hide my awe. The house was bigger than the size of two shotgun houses placed one on top of the other. Shot gun houses are houses that run in a straight line with each room following the next. They have their charm, but I was determined to live in a house much bigger one day. A house like Beth's blue one.

"It's over a hundred years old and needs tons of work, so we don't mind trashing it every once in awhile. You'll see when you come for the party. From far away it looks like a palace but up close, it's just your ordinary Brady house." But, the Brady's were *not* ordinary. They were a sitcom family full of repressed issues.

I told the cab driver I would get out too. I could walk through campus. The fare was six dollars each and hardly dented our pockets. I paid the driver in quarters. He glared at me disapprovingly. "You think I'm a slot machine? We a long way from Vegas child."

I imitated his accent. "I prolly have ten more dollars in quarters if you want a better tip. Besides, I thought emulating the slot machine payoff was supposed to be a thrill."

"Go on. Git."

***

I hoped the Dorm Nerd was asleep at four-fifty-four a.m. I tiptoed up two flights of steps and found a note on my door. I ripped it off and tried to unlock the door, but the key wouldn't fit. *The prick had changed the locks on me?*

I opened the note. 'Please be advised that your strenuous efforts to disobey orders have resulted in the changing of your locks. It is highly recommended you now make alternate living arrangements. Your current fine is approximately three hundred dollars.' He signed it "Enrique, interim resident advisor."

"Can you hear me asshole? I'm not paying this." I began to scream. Three hundred dollars would be a rent payment. Staying in the dorm would cost me more than I thought it was saving me. Couldn't he be a little more compassionate? He was probably on some form of financial aid too, since he got stuck with this shitty ass job. *Wait.* Maybe he thought I was Jackson.

I heard a door above me slam and Enrique's footsteps on the stairs. This was one of those times I wished I had a boyfriend. He could kick this punk's ass.

Enrique stood before me. I didn't recognize the stand-in for my normal resident advisor. He was a shrimp sized boy that looked younger than me. I didn't need a boyfriend. I could kick this guy's ass. My gaydar beeped loudly.

"You're trespassing young lady."

"I live here. Let me in."

"I'm afraid you were supposed to vacate the premises until January 13ᵗʰ Miss, Miss…."

He looked at the number on the room I had left and then back at his clipboard. "What's your name, Calina or Jackson?"

Hmm. It's not that I wanted to get Jackson in trouble. I was just sick of her spoiled behavior and the pressure and distance she made me feel when I wanted to choose studying over partying with her. Maybe if she was fined and didn't know why, she would depend on me to figure it out. Then she would be grateful.

I also wanted Dorm Nerd to screw up his job. Jackson would certainly go ballistic on the school when her parents accused her of being irresponsible for allowing the school to make the mistake of charging money on their bank account. I thought rich people didn't notice insignificant charges, but the Miltons scrutinized their bills.

Ultimately, it was Dorm Nerd's own fault. He should have known that Jackson didn't need to stay here. I pointed to her name on our door.

"I knew it! Miss Jackson, I will repeat. You aren't allowed to be here. I don't know why you insist on breaking the rules. Perhaps a family squabble?"

"It's Miss Milton to you. Just let me sleep here one night. I'm tired. I've been working all night." He should know Jackson would never need a job.

"You can afford a hotel room with all that family bar money." So he *did* know, but if he was *really* in the gossip ring around school, he would know that one of the club heiress' best friends was her dirt poor roommate.

"Too many fines can result in school suspension."

He should know Jackson could buy her way back into school. I could see the ultimate irony now, the Milton School of Business, or laziness in her case.

He was making this difficult, but I didn't like how he was talking to Jackson. I didn't agree with Jackson and some of her snooty friends' behavior towards less fortunate people, but I also didn't think poor people had a right to be rude to people just because they had money. The one thing I remember my real mother saying was that two wrongs don't make a right.

"You took property that didn't belong to you. That's worse than sleeping in a dorm when you aren't supposed to."

"Miss Milton, I don't know what you're talking about."

"I saw you take my Madonna CD yesterday."

He laughed. "You must be on the drugs seeing things."

"I know you have it."

"I was only listening to that. I was going to put it back. You must still go."

"I need my apparel." Something Jackson would say. At least I was in character.

"Can't you buy more?"

I decided to continue my role. "Daddy froze my account." I whined. "Whatever will I do?" Enrique pouted and unlocked the door.

As I headed to my closet he eyed me. "You don't have to watch me. I know how to pack a suitcase."

"Just want to make sure you take what is yours only. Your recent bad luck might make you do something silly like other socialites in trouble. We all know the Patty Hearst story."

I scowled. "I didn't get kidnapped by a cult. And I'm not being forced to rob a bank."

"She still knew what she was doing." Enrique huffed. "Hurry up."

I bid Enrique farewell with a final statement. The one thing Jackson and I had in common was our second language of French. "I attended La Baie des Anges Academy in St. Tropez. Fun, sun, shopping and sex. We would get other people to rob the banks."

All my belongings packed in two suitcases Jackson called stewardess bags, I wheeled them through campus and to the only place where I thought someone would still be awake.

***

Ten minutes later, I arrived. The house had an eerie quality at night. Audubon Park hovered in the pitch black, full of trees with Spanish moss swaying like hands ready to grab and strangle. The porch lights were all off. I knocked on the door hoping the park wouldn't swallow me before someone answered.

A sleepy faced Beth answered the door. "Calina, what are you doing here?"

"I'm sorry. I didn't know where else to go. I got kicked out of the dorms."

"Oh, come in sweetie. You're welcome here."

The sweetie word didn't bother me at this moment. "Sorry for waking you up."

"No problem. I told you earlier I'm normally awake and still out at this time. My boyfriend's over, but I have a futon in my room. You can crash and then we can move it into your own room tomorrow."

"My own room?"

"Our roommate disappeared. We have plenty of space here."

That's sketchy, I thought. However, I wasn't about to object to living in a house only an hour ago, I was aspiring to have one day in the *very* distant future.

I stepped inside and couldn't see to the end of the house like I normally could in a shotgun. We walked up a flight of stairs that rounded a corner. There were two doors on the right, and we turned the corner and took a left to Beth's room. Another room was across from it.

Once in the bedroom, I whispered, "I don't think I can pay rent yet."

"No sweat sweetie." Jesus, she created a bad alliteration always throwing in her sweetie. "I wasn't expecting it. We'll work something out."

I felt guilty for being so rude to Beth in the library. But I also knew nothing in life was for free.

***

I woke to pounding footsteps on the hardwood floor. Many New Orleans houses wisely lacked carpeting. The door flew open and someone turned on the bright lights as I threw the covers over my head. I hated people seeing me in the morning. "Time to get up Beth. You lazy, drunk bitch."

I recognized that voice. Beth stirred and sat up, and I peaked from under my blanket. I saw Darla, the cocktail waitress who demonstrated how to do a body shot. She stood in the doorway fiddling with her lip and making repetitive sniffle sounds. It wasn't hard to spot the drug within her. It was as if I was peering into her heart and could see it stained white. Oh lovely, I thought. In walks the poster child for a 1980's coke addict.

Darla began to speak. Fast.

"Hey, I know you. You bringing home strays Beth?" She turned towards me. "It used to be animals, now it's people."

"Can't you see we were sleeping Darla?" Beth sat up and threw a pillow at her roommate. "And I found good homes for those animals."

Great, now I'm a pet.

"Fine. I'm off to clean, clean, clean. Do we have any Mr. Clean? I think I'll mop."

Darla shut the door. I was going to have to live with her? *Please god, send me a money angel.*

Beth laid back down and curled up next to her unseen boyfriend saying for my benefit, "It'll wear off soon, and then she'll sleep. At least it gets her to do her chores. Don't worry. It's kind of funny sometimes."

Funny? I wanted a normal life. Stable. Together. I could see I wasn't going to get it anytime soon. Maybe I would sleep some more and wake up with a new life.

An hour later it was still the same. I lay in bed and heard a muffled voice ask, "Is it time to get up already?"

Beth answered her boyfriend. "No sweetie. You can sleep longer." I heard her kiss him and felt awkward. What if they wanted to do it?

I rose and left to look around my new house. I began in the living room. All the furniture was from Pottery Barn. They had a surround sound television system with a DVD player. Those were fairly new and expensive. The kitchen was filled with William Sonoma cutlery. I had walked through these stores before at Canal Place Shops and fantasized how when I got married, I would register for all the great kitchen and house wares.

I was thinking about how Beth and Darla could possibly afford all of these nice things when Darla stumbled into the living room. She hadn't come down from her drugs, but was a little less hyper.

"Hey, new girl. I forgot your name."

"Calina."

"Right. You gonna be our new roommate?"

I shook my head yes, and Darla told me to come see her room. Again, I saw another room of expensive furniture. She had a waterbed. I had never been on one before, but I heard they were bad for your back. I took a chance. The rocking felt like what I thought floating on a raft in the ocean must be like. I could have laid there all day. She showed me her closet and told me I could borrow, but to ask first just in case she needed anything.

"Really?"

"Of course." Darla laughed like it was silly to think otherwise. I sifted through the dresses. A Betsy Johnson dress. A Bebe dress. A Nicole Miller dress. She must have wealthy parents like Jackson. Only, they must have taught her how to share. She couldn't possibly afford all of these amazing things with her Black

Sevens money, could she? Maybe she had a sugar daddy or maybe Beth's stripping had led them into a world of prostitution. No, they both seemed too picky to fuck just anyone. *What was the catch?*

Darla went to take a shower and I headed back downstairs to check out the television. "Did you sleep okay?" Beth asked from behind my shoulder.

"The futon beat my closet floor."

"You poor thing." Poor was right, and I was determined to find the secrets to their wallets.

Chapter 5

The rest of the day, I put my clothes on my new closet shelves and then hung out with Beth and watched her get ready for work. She had the early evening and night shifts today. She sat before a mirror and brushed her *real,* long hair. She was movie star beautiful and normally dressed casual, yet chic, pairing jeans with preppy tops and heels.

Beth explained that her boyfriend had left when I was in Darla's room, and that he wasn't that social sometimes. In the daylight, I saw that her room was just as nice as Darla's. I wanted to get her something nice for all of her help. I noticed she was low on the scented lotion sitting on her vanity. Before work, I would go to Bath and Body Works and get her one of those gift packs consisting of the lotion, the shower gel and the spray.

I went on my quest to RiverWalk, a mall situated downtown on the crescent shaped Mississippi River. A year before, I had planned to go with a friend, but luckily, I got sick. A 700-foot freighter registered to Liberia crashed into the mall and tore into a 200-foot section of the mall's walkway, damaging 13-15 stores and some condos. Among the damage was a collapsed building containing a 125- room hotel and a parking garage. Maybe there *was* a higher power on my side.

I wandered through Bath and Body Works and somehow, a duplicate lotion and bath set was purchased. I needed it to smell good for work, I justified. After I was finished, I headed to Dick's Palace to drop off Beth's present on the way to Black Sevens.

I entered the lobby after a twenty minute walk, and a girl stopped me. "Can I help you?"

"My roommate works here. I just want to drop something off for her. I work over at Black Sevens." I hadn't changed into my uniform yet and thought if she knew I worked on the street, maybe it would give me some credibility.

"What's her name?"

"Beth. I mean, Celexa."

"Sometimes we get angry wives looking for husbands, so I had to make sure you weren't lyin. Go on in. I think she's on the floor." *Did I look old enough to be someone's wife already?* Had my nomadic life made me look older than my age? People usually thought I was sixteen. This girl was just dumb, I told myself.

"Thanks." I uttered through my teeth with a hint of sarcasm.

I entered the dimly lit room with many stages. Little white lights illuminated the stages to give the customers a better, brighter view of the show. Although every shape, size and color danced on the various stages, I couldn't help but feel a little out of place in clothing.

I stared at the cocktail waitresses by the bar. I made my way over to one waitress who was busy tapping drink orders into a computer screen with her finger. "Excuse me, have you seen Celexa?"

She hollered to the bartender. "The goddamn squirrel ain't working again."

The computer was named after a rodent? I was suddenly very happy I worked in a different club. We didn't have to do any high maintenance work. We just told the bartender what we wanted, and they took care of the rest. Besides the pain in the ass computer entry, the waitresses all looked like they had boob jobs, and they wore the worst outfit. A black, silver studded bra, a translucent silver shirt tied at their midriffs, those bloomers that cheerleaders wear under their skirts, and black stockings. What an awful, half-naked concoction.

I repeated my question to the angry waitress. "Have you seen Celexa?"

She answered without even looking at me. "She'll be on in a minute."

The song playing changed to The Buggles, *Video Killed The Radio Star*, and I turned around to face the main stage. I knew who loved that song, because I had heard it playing a few times before I left the house today. Celexa was one of those girls that overplayed a song and then suddenly got sick of it and discarded it.

I hoped she didn't act that way towards her roommates. Who *really* knew why the old roommate disappeared.

My mouth dropped as she came out wearing a catholic school girl outfit and proceeded to dance and take off all her clothes until she was down to her red thong with a heart on the butt crack. I couldn't really blame her for the decorative undies, because I had some with smiley faces. At least *she* had an excuse.

Celexa must have enjoyed Abba's *Dancing Queen* as much as DJ Ray-Ray, but she added a word in front of the song title: *Naked.* Suddenly, I was watching her simulate sex with dirty old men, and the reality of her job hit me along with the reality of the new world I had entered.

Although I had lived close by for two and a half years due to my time with the Holts, Bourbon Street was a whole different scene from my daily, newly sheltered world in New Orleans. The library, studying, and partying with rich friends and frat boys suddenly vanished and were replaced by naked bodies with orange tinted tans, lots of visible displays of money, and shady characters. A day really did make a difference.

I suddenly felt cheap. A slut to money instead of sex. But wait, sluts to sex are in it for the money. Either way, it's a paradoxical feeling. Dirty, but good, knowing one way or another I would leave the street with money.

Celexa saw me in the crowd and signaled for me to come closer. I stood at the edge of the stage, and she danced towards me. She leaned in and kissed me on the lips, the men screaming and clapping. I suddenly realized why she chose to name her dancing self after an anti-depressant. She served as one to these lonely men.

Examining the scene, it was a life away from a frat party, yet in some respects very similar in that those guys would have loved the girl on girl action. Bourbon Street was a classier version of a world I had briefly witnessed living with foster mom Jacky, the coke whore. I called her Cracky instead. She was also a stripper, but danced in the local mom and pop strip club.

At least I knew Celexa wouldn't be bringing men home since she had a boyfriend. And, she seemed a lot shrewder with men than Cracky Jacky.

Celexa whispered, "I'll be off in two sets." I waited by the bar to avoid the men who stared at me. I feared they would ask me to dance.

Celexa danced to the Goo Goo Dolls' *Iris* next. The chorus sang, "And I don't want the world to see me, cause I don't think that they'd understand, when everything's made to be broken, I just want you to know who I am." *She's got some issues,* I thought. The next song, The Smith's *How Soon is Now*, was just as telling. "I go about things the wrong way. I am human and I need to be loved, just like everybody else does." I wanted attention too, but I wasn't about to take my clothes off for it. After her songs, she disappeared behind the curtain.

She approached me in a skimpy, slinky Frederick's of Hollywood slip. I think it had some kind of miracle type push up bra because her normal A cups looked like C cups. "You'd see me around the house half naked anyway, so I guess we got it out of the way."

I must have squinted my forehead like I did when I had more questions because Celexa continued to inform me about her life as a nude dancing queen.

"I started dancing when I was your age. I'm twenty-eight now, and they'll probably get rid of me one of these days and tell me I'm too old and wrinkly. Although, we do have a forty-year-old who does tricks with bottles in her routine. She was on the Travel Channel talking about it once when they did a special on New Orleans. I'm getting sick of this life anyway. That's why I finally went back to school. I've got to go work the club for lap dances now."

Before Celexa left, I handed her the present. She loved it. I could imagine the fruity scent suiting both her personalities.

When I entered Black Sevens a few minutes later, I saw Round Randy approach a nearby young black man with gold teeth leaning against a railing where people placed empty beer bottles. He was one of the boys from the projects who the club hired to sweep and clean the bar railings. He gawked at some half-dressed drunken girls dancing on stage. Except for them, the club was empty. I waved to Chucky as I passed by him and heard Round Randy ask him, "Hey Chucky, you got stuff to clean?"

"Naw, I already does it."

Round Randy took an empty beer bottle and threw it on the ground, shattering glass everywhere. "You got time to lean, you got time to clean."

Several people laughed and Chucky sauntered away for a mop. Round Randy was such an ass.

As I headed up the stairs, I hoped Will was working. I heard someone talking. "My nephew is taking care of everything."

I stood at the doorway as Will said, "I don't care. I do my part, and that's it."

The man nodded at Will and turned to leave. He passed by me and didn't even glance my way.

"Who was that?" I asked Will.

"That's Paul. He owns the club, but he doesn't come around that often. Watches the monitors from home when he feels like it."

The owner. That might explain the superior attitude. His snub was different than Jackson's sorority sisters. He just didn't give a rat's ass about his employees at the bottom of the ladder. Like Will had told me, frequent turnaround. I guessed he felt comfortable with how his management staff ran the club. I had learned in my Entrepreneurial Management class that when you had your own business, you needed to keep a keen eye on it. People might steal from you, if you weren't careful.

I had already applied the concept in foster care. The biological children always stole things from me. I always left to go to the next home with nothing. Even my favorite stuffed animals got left behind. Taken away. I never had something to hold onto. And I wanted something, anything, long lasting.

Love and comfort were secondary to money, and I broke from my rumination. I had to think of the present. I had to get back into school. Maybe once I finished school, I would run my own club like this Paul character.

After traveling around the club a few times, I rested my tray on a free table. My back hurt a little from the night before. My attempts at weight lifting must be pretty shoddy cause the tray was pretty heavy to me. I stared down at my sneakers when two feet slightly more than twice my own size seven feet stood a centimeter from mine.

I looked up as he asked for shots and put a face with the feet. Staring into his blue eyes, I thought I might as well be permanently placed on a microwave safe tray to rotate around with defrosting food. I melted as I handed him his shot request. He stared at my nametag. As a tourist club, they certainly had good promotions. Pens, shirts, and of course, the pins that displayed our names.

"Calina. Is that your real name?" He asked.

I nodded, and he told me his name was Jim. I took the bill he handed me. Before I placed his tip in my black apron, I looked at it to avoid staring at him. "I can't accept this." *Sure I could.*

"Play innocent sometimes." Celexa had also given me those words of wisdom in the taxi the night before. *Should I really be taking advice from her?* I guess she knew how to get money from men, but I certainly didn't want to end up working with her.

Jim had given me a twenty in addition to what he already paid for the shots. They cost two dollars each and he bought three. The tip was over two hundred percent.

"Keep it." I thanked him. The dimples on his left cheek made his smile appear like a little boy's innocent, but conniving look when he has done something wrong and doesn't want Mommy and Daddy to find out.

"What time do you get off?"

"Never." Celexa had also said you should play with the customers. The happier you made them, the more money in your pocket.

"We're making our way down the street, and I thought you might want to join us after your shift." He pointed at his unenthusiastic friends Josh, a short and pudgy guy and Eli, a pimple faced lanky guy. Jim was the gem of this trio.

"Why would you think that?" He had just tipped well, so I had to be careful not to offend him with my sarcasm.

"You looked pretty bored when that guy did a body shot."

"So you've been watching me?"

"You *are* the best looking girl I've ever seen in here."

"A regular, huh? Well, I have to study for my final tonight."

"After work? It's almost January. Don't schools have Winter Break?"

"I mean my pre-term."

"A what?"

"You know, an exam to see what we already know. I have to keep moving or my bosses will yell at me." I had the upper hand. This time. "Let me know if you need drinks or more shots."

"Actually, I would like a Jack and Coke."

When I returned with his drink, Jim gave me a hundred percent tip. "Are you trying to point the way out?" He asked.

"What do you mean?"

"The compass in the drink. It's pointing towards the door."

I laughed. The club had been putting little fake, plastic compasses in the drinks tonight. Clubs on Bourbon Street liked to make customers feel as if they were getting a free toy with their purchase like a McDonald's happy meal. Making adults feel like kids. They certainly acted like them once the alcohol seeped into their bloodstream.

At two-forty-five a.m., I finished selling my last tray and headed upstairs to finish my shift. Round Randy sat at the checkout desk. He counted my money. "Grab another tray."

"What? I'm done. My shift is almost over."

"Finish another tray for me before you leave if you want to keep your job."

What an ass. I would be stuck at the club for at least another hour. I headed to the refrigerator for another tray.

I spotted Will standing near the back of the club talking to a guy wearing a black leather jacket and torn jeans. The man's inflection made me think he was annoyed. I walked closer so I could wait for Will, and got a better look. The guy had dark, shaggy, chin length hair, but green eyes and a weird birthmark on his cheek. He looked around Beth's age or a little older.

"Look, we're doing it through the beer tub. Don't worry. You're paranoid. You need to chill the fuck out man."

"Don't tell me to chill. I'm trying to understand." His voice sounded familiar, but I couldn't place it.

"What happens is I close out the register and then reopen it."

Will saw me staring at them. "If you'll excuse me, I got a club to run." He walked away, and the guy headed for what I thought must be the back entrance.

"Owner's nephew?"

"No, why you think that?"

I had heard the owner talk about his nephew earlier and assumed. Before I could answer, Will continued, "That guy is scum. Stay away from guys like him." He stared at me. "Why you pouting?"

"Do y'all always make us take out another tray when our shift is almost over? Does it really matter to y'all how many shots the club sells?" My southern accent slipped out when I was annoyed.

"Randy can be a jerk. Just do the best you can."

I realized my teachers in elementary school had lied. There was such thing as a stupid question. The managers were probably receiving some kind of incentive for how much alcohol was sold during their shifts, just like the cocktail waitresses.

At four a.m., I threw the money down on the desk in front of Round Randy. "Now was that so bad?" He asked. I ignored him and went to change into jeans and a more comfortable top. I came downstairs and sat at the patio bar where Will stood behind the register.

"How much money did you make, darlin?"

"Two fifty." I answered happily.

For seven hours of work, I made more money than most people did at a normal job. I could get addicted to this money. I gloated, thinking about the fabricated power it gave me. I could buy one of those designer bags the sorority girls from my school carried.

I imagined winking at them and pissing them off as I walked by. But then, my thoughts of sweet revenge were shattered by images of rent, school, food, and clothing. Accessories were something I could do without. I knew my own self-worth wasn't dictated by material items, yet I still wanted what everyone else around me had.

I watched Will pull the tape from the register. I fantasized about what I could do with all that money. For starters, pay for school. It would be nice to always have money in an account, like a safety net. You could live within a range, yet if you really wanted something badly, you could have it and never be in trouble.

I asked Will, "how much money has the club made so far?" He loved to talk business so I knew he would tell me.

"Around thirty thousand."

"Wow. I thought it was a slow night."

"You made good money, then it ain't slow." His tone was matter of fact, but there was an annoyance in his voice. Maybe he was sick of dealing with people after the scummy guy.

"I'm not complaining." I answered.

I was just trying to understand how the number for the club was *that* high. It wasn't the weekend yet, and no big conventions were in town. I didn't do stellar in my finance class, but wow. I said nothing, assuming I was wrong.

Will was the manager. He knew what he was doing. But I only made good money because I had a few big tippers, Jim included. Otherwise, I might have left with much less. I got jealous that the business made so much more than I did, even though I knew I was a minor player. I obsessed how I could put my profits in the black.

I said goodnight to Will and headed towards the front door. Jim stopped me. "Going out with us now? We've been waiting all night for you."

"I don't hang out with customers."

"Aww. That's not cool. Come on."

"I'm tired. You weren't the one walking around crazy, drunk people all night."

"At least give me your phone number, so we can hang out some other time."

Sure, if it would get this guy off my back so I could go home harassment free. I scribbled a phone number on a napkin with my Black Sevens pen. Jim raised my hand to his mouth and kissed it when I gave him the napkin. *Was he for real?*

As I walked through the exit of the club, I heard Will tell him, "You shouldn't hang out here so much. Go home. And don't harass my workers." I couldn't decipher if Will's tone was another case of being annoyed with people or if he knew Jim well.

Chapter 6

The sunlight coming through my giant sized window woke me. After I yawned and stretched, I rose and walked onto the balcony overlooking Audubon Park. I watched athletes run on the track and owners play Frisbee with their dogs. Occasionally the owners would stop to chat with other pet owners, most likely I presumed, exchanging niceties about which pedigree the animal belonged to.

Waking to this picturesque view sure beat the noise of the trucks and workers that delivered food to the cafeteria next to my former dorm. I couldn't believe Jackson slummed it. I could see myself living in this house for a very long time.

I peered in the window adjacent to mine to determine if Darla was awake in her bedroom. She only worked at the club two times a week, so I wasn't worried about seeing her too often there and at home and getting sick of her. I didn't know if she needed the money or if it was just to pass some time since she only took three classes a semester. Beth said Darla's parents gave her an allowance, but she always used it to shop for clothes the first week the check came in the mail.

If I got a check in the mail each week, I'd feel like there was a god looking down on me. Maybe Darla worked to afford the amenities in the house and the plethora of clothing purchases in her closet. They were beyond an allowance.

Through the opaque blinds, her room was still, and she wasn't in her bed. She was probably still partying somewhere. With the free time I would have while not being in school, I needed some way to pass the time. I decided I would go take a kickboxing class at Kung Fu For Yu on Magazine Street. Beth had told me they were eight dollars a class. I could afford it with my current club money. After all, I had to stay in shape for work, I justified.

The class at Kung Fu For Yu was better than the University Fitness Center's class because the instructors challenged us more by yelling in our faces to push harder. Kickboxing gave me a sense of control and empowerment since no other area in my life did. Maybe, if I handled my finances right, I could go more than once a week to occupy myself.

After an hour of back, side, and front kicks, jabs, and undercuts, I felt an overwhelming depletion of energy that made me want to put my head on a pillow and sleep for hours. I walked downstairs like a zombie, slow and methodical, PJ's Coffee Shop calling my name.

Standing in line, I spotted Jim, the guy I met at Black Sevens the night before. I heard him order a plain coffee, no famous chicory added. I pulled the rubber band out of my hair and let it fall loosely around my face, moving more strands in front of my left side that faced the walkway as opposed to the counter. I hoped he wouldn't recognize me.

"Calina?" *Shit. Too late.* I stopped messing with my hair and pulled it back. He offered to buy my coffee. We awkwardly waited for my iced mocha and then, I followed him outside to a table. I hoped this wouldn't be uncomfortable.

"I just worked out, so I probably look a mess."

"Guys like to see girls sweaty. But why would you care how you look? I talked to an older gentleman this morning who called himself Percy."

"I'm sorry." I felt like a jerk. He had been a good tipper, and I made up the number I gave him. I explained I had to protect myself from the crazies on Bourbon Street. Some of them reminded me of people from back home.

"You don't have to apologize. I have a date with him tomorrow."

I laughed.

"I knew I would see you again and get you to break your no hanging out with customers rule." That was cocky, I thought. But then he added, "It was easy. You're already doing it by having coffee with me."

I relaxed. Maybe he wasn't as egotistical as I had first thought he would be because of his looks. I admitted to myself that I needed to revise my tendency to judge people too quickly.

"Besides, I think it's really good that you don't wander off with strange men. I called you to apologize if I was too annoying. I rarely drink, and I had one too many."

"So then, you had goggle eyes for me?"

"Um, no. The attraction is real."

I blushed at his directness and asked him how often he hung out at Black Sevens. "Only a few times. I like the music." Jim told me about his love for hip-hop. The conversation switched to our common interests in athletic activities. He told me he would take me to a rock climbing gym sometime, since that was the next activity I wanted to master.

When we switched to discussing movies, Jim told me his favorite was *Star Wars* and that he saw it in the theater when he was five. I calculated quickly and realized that Jim was not the same age as me, despite his young appearance.

He saw my contemplation. "I'm 27." Being older by eight years made him more appealing to me. It meant he might not be as immature as the college frat boys.

My frat boy experiences were never high quality. They always tried to push more alcohol to get me drunk and take advantage of me. I saw right through it, but I knew all men weren't the same as foster dad number two. One woman wasn't enough for him.

Our trips to pick up groceries always ended in my sitting in the back seat of the car while he visited a, "friend," inside a house.

I was a wise kid and knew his, "friends," were really mistresses. Needless to say there were no pints of ice cream in those grocery bags. Nor eggs, milk, cheese, or anything else that would spoil. So that's why I ate as much ice cream as I wanted now. At least he gave me magic middle cookies while I waited. I wanted to thank those Keebler Elves for keeping me busy in the car. I always took my time with those cookies. A bite, a lick of the chocolate inside. By the time we made it home, and mother number two tried to make me eat dinner, I was full.

Now, those cookies make me ill. But even though my relationship with men followed the same path as my cookie eating habits, I just hadn't met the right one.

I did sample a few frat boys and other guys from school just like I eventually tried other brands of cookies, but after the spark fizzled, usually due to their aspirations to smoke pot all day, guzzle beer all night, or a combination of both, I had decided I would never have a boyfriend in college. Maybe Jim would be the cookie that sparked a new craving.

I decided it wouldn't hurt to give Jim a try. I glanced at my watch, remembering I had to be at work. "I've got to head home now and shower. Thanks for the coffee. If you still want my number, I'll give you the real one." I waited for his answer, my nails digging into the paper coffee cup in anticipation he would reject me for my earlier deceit.

"I'll call you, as long as you pick up instead of Percy." I smiled and began to walk towards the streetcar. I wondered if Jim would be the right cookie.

***

The next afternoon, Darla and Beth insisted I shop with them. "Where are we going?" I asked.

"Walmart, the mall."

I loved big stores where you could find various products all under one roof. Maybe I would buy some candles for my room. We piled into Beth's white Grand Jeep Cherokee and headed around St. Charles Avenue to Carrolton Ave. to hit the I-10. I liked her car, but I would be happy for even a piece of junk to transport me.

Darla had totaled her car and lost her license due to a D.U.I. A lawyer representing all the University students when they were, "bad," argued that she should only lose it for three months. The judge agreed. The lawyer contributed to the judge's re-election campaigns. Gotta love New Orleans.

Twenty minutes later, I wandered through the bath section of Walmart, smelling candles to determine if they would actually give off a strong scent when lit. I decided on lavender for its promise to relax. Darla rounded the corner and picked up a peppermint candle. Figured. Its scent offered to stimulate.

I followed Darla over to the kitchenware section where Beth stood examining Bread Makers. Fresh smells of apple pie, chocolate chip cookies, and banana bread still reminded me of my birth mother. She lived and died baking. Literally. There was a gas leak. I was at school in kindergarten.

Beth decided against the bread maker. "Domesticity still isn't my thing no matter how much I try. Cal, I saw some great furniture for you." She took my hand and led me through the store. "You need a real room."

"It has four walls. Seems like one to me."

"I mean one with a dresser, a night stand, a TV. We'll get you a bed from Mattress World later."

"What's wrong with what's in the room now?"

"It's too masculine. Our old roommate was a dude."

I didn't want to complain to her that I couldn't afford all new furniture. I really wanted to make my new home last. I had this shattered hope so many times before, that I felt destined to remain a gypsy.

"Let me see how much money is in my account." I reached into my purse and pulled out my checkbook register. We didn't have online banking in the late 90s. We couldn't just check our accounts on our mobile devices.

When I was ten, I used to play with my neighbor, Melissa, in her tree house. She had two years of age and wisdom on me and taught me about saving when I told her I might run away and build my own house in the trees to live in all by myself. Then, I wouldn't have to listen to foster dad Arnie tell my foster mom Kelly that she was infertile because her insides were damaged from being a whore. I knew from his tone of voice and his hand slapping against Kelly's face, that a whore wasn't something desirable.

And best of all, I wouldn't have to see him drag her out into the yard and pour bird seed into the yard and make her crawl on all fours and lick it up. He even sprinkled it on the dog poop that flies were feeding on. He made her lick all the birdseed up, whether it rested on the poop or not. Then he made her ask for forgiveness from god. If licking up animal food and feces was the way to make peace with god, I preferred hell.

Melissa's response to my plan of escape was saving. Not from evil, but from myself. She said I could never run away if I had no money. Anytime I got some extra money, she said, I should hide it and make my own personal bank. When the time was right, I would have a small fortune.

My first opportunity to save presented itself when Arnie decided we shouldn't pay the bills. He thought we should live in darkness because electricity was an unnatural evil, invented by a messenger of the devil to tempt us. Although, if someone else paid the bill, Arnie would allow the lights.

Kelly would give me cash and tell me to run on down the street and pay it. She told Arnie her father was paying the bill. A few times, I kept the money and hid it for my personal account.

When the lights didn't come back on, I told Kelly I had been mugged. Other inventions followed this, such as it fell down the drainpipe when I tripped on a rock. I even scrapped myself with rocks to make it look more authentic. I wasn't stealing from my own mom, I told myself. I was saving for my uncertain future.

I didn't need Darwin to learn about survival of the fittest, but I guess my penchant for science developed at this time. I couldn't rely on Kelly and Arnie for survival. I never did run away because I was moved when Arnie lit Kelly on fire as an offering to save her from damnation.

I did learn saving was hard. At each house I subtracted what I had before and tried to play a game to see if I could leave with more. I always seemed to leave with less. Life costs got in the way. I wanted this New Year to be different. Maybe I could finally save something. Although, it would be gone when I paid for school. There's that life cost thing again.

Beth jolted me back to the present by snatching the checkbook register out of my hands and examining it. "You're a worry wart. Now, I think this will look great." She pointed at a glass top nightstand with black wrought iron legs. "It's very Pier Oneish and it's much cheaper to make you feel better." She sounded like a salesgirl trying to make a pitch. Although, she knew she wouldn't get any commission from me.

When we got to electronics, I eyed a TV/VCR combo. What the heck, I'll make the money back. But when we got to the register, I wanted to puke. It seemed like a waste since I wasn't drunk with happy thoughts, but intoxicated with worry. My breathing became shallow. The bill was six hundred dollars. There goes my whole savings account. I didn't feel like Jackson buying whatever I wanted, but like orphan Annie, pre-Daddy Warbucks.

In the car, Darla begged Beth, "Let's go to Canal Place Shops. Pleaseeee." We rode to the French Quarter on the other side of town. I had not done this much shopping in my entire life. At least this leg of the trip I would just watch. I rested my head against the window to take a power nap. Spending money was exhausting.

We went to Saks and Betsy Johnson during the remainder of our shopping excursion. To me, a shopping spree was a trip to the Goodwill store and an occasional trip to a bigger city for Express or The Gap. Not to these two fashionistas who had every fashion magazine possible from around the world displayed on our coffee table.

Darla coerced me to try on some jeans. I needed a new wardrobe, she said. Beth waved a black cocktail dress in front of my face. I couldn't afford either, but they convinced me. Both items could be worn so many times they would pay for themselves. "It's like dollar cost averaging." Beth justified as she walked with them to the register, reminding me of the term I had learned in a business class regarding purchasing stocks.

If you bought a stock at a high price and the stock fell, you could buy more at the lower price. Then, as the stock rises again you can say your average cost of buying the stock is lowered.

"Not exactly. One of the items would have to be on sale. Where did you learn that term?" I asked her.

"I read the Wall Street Journal. My father was a businessman before he retired. My first word was stock instead of Mom or Dad. It might not be dollar cost averaging, but divide the amount of times you will wear each piece by its cost and then they will seem much cheaper."

Her suggestion did make the items more appealing. At one hundred dollars for the jeans, if I wore them one hundred times in a year they would be a dollar each time. The salesgirl rang up the clothes. I put my hands over my eyes, but that didn't make the price of 300 dollars go away.

Beth handed her a black card and the salesgirl eyed Beth suspiciously. "Can I see some I.D. please?"

Beth slapped her I.D. down. "Do I look like a criminal?" She asked. Her eyes narrowed and I hadn't seen her pissed before.

The saleswoman examined her I.D. "I'm sorry, it's just policy. Normally we have older men and, she whispered and made air quotes, "rap stars," using this."

"Well, I'm a V.I.P." When we walked away, I asked Beth what that interaction was all about. "The Visa Black Card has no limit."

"Wow."

"I always dance in the section where men must purchase a 300-dollar bottle of champagne to even enter. It's called the V.I.P. section."

We both laughed. I figured her Dad must be on the card too, but then she said she was the primary cardholder. She could charge ten thousand worth of clothes and make it back fast.

My anxiety came back. I told her, "I'll never get back to school. Maybe I should dance." I was kidding, yet I knew there was always some truth to a joke.

"I would never let you dance, Calina." The tone in Beth's voice reminded me of Arnie's. If I didn't obey him, I would risk being sent to eat from the yard like Kelly. Kelly had no more gag reflex. At least I would be great in bed.

Beth noticed my slight flinch and softened her voice to explain, "I mean, anything is better than prostituting your body in front of men. I bet you didn't realize, but most of those strippers are jaded. About half become lesbians."

We greeted Darla who was smiling at herself in the MAC make-up counter mirror, and we finally left for home.

Chapter 7

New Year's Eve day, I threw on my new jeans, courtesy of Beth, and went downstairs for breakfast. I owed her, "big money," as I used to hear contestants on the *Price Is Right*, wish aloud for as they spun the wheel. I hated owing.

As I headed down the stairs, I smelled potpourri boiling on the stove. At the bottom of the steps, I looked up to see streamers of blue, white, and silver flowing from the staircase back up to the ceiling.

Taking a few steps into the foyer, I saw balloons throughout the other rooms, the same colors of the streamers, floating on the ceiling. Others saying Happy New Year with reverse text of white letters on a black background were tied to a few different chairs.

In the kitchen, unopened bags of chips and closed containers of cookies and liquor lined the table and bar. I thought it must be like the kiddie b-day extravaganza I never had. Too bad I was scheduled to work. It seemed to me any party in this house was bound to be interesting.

I spotted Beth in the kitchen hanging more streamers. "I forgot the noise makers, Cal. Do you think you could take my car and make a run to Party Town? You're a decent driver, right? I don't trust Darla, and she's out cold."

Let's see. I possessed a license that maybe got used twice a year since I entered college, and maybe twenty days out of 364 the two years before that. "I'm not very seasoned."

"Oh, I'm sure you'll be cautious and safe. It'll give you some practice. Maybe you'll even have a car of your own soon."

"I wouldn't count on it. Speaking of money, I have to leave for work soon."

"Change of plans. You don't have to work. And don't be so pessimistic all the time. The world is open to you."

"Why don't I have to work?" I asked, as I thought the world is really open to people with money.

"I asked Will if you could have off to attend our party. Surprise."

"Why did you do that without asking me? I need the money bad. I owe you 300 dollars."

"I'm not worried about that, Cal." Beth was never concerned about money. It must be nice, but how could she constantly shell out the dough? She didn't dance *that* many nights.

She continued to appease me. "Cal, if you are *that* worried about money, I'll send you on some errands for me after the New Year. Then, you will owe me nothing. Don't be such a drag on New Years. The party will be much more fun than walking around that tourist bar. You might meet a nice, professional man tonight. Here are my keys."

Take a deep breath, I told myself. Remember when I was about to become homeless a week ago, and Beth took me in. That all worked out. So would this.

I grabbed the keys out of her hand and headed for the door. I realized she was trying to do me what she thought was a favor, but I needed the money. I hated people going behind my back. It felt like foster care all over again. Never knowing when someone will pluck you out of one place and put you in another.

And what were these errands she would send me on? Did she want me to be her personal assistant? Still, that was nice she would not make me pay her for the clothes if I ran some errands. I would do *almost* anything for her since she took me in.

When I returned an hour later with the noisemakers and a dent free car, Darla sat at the kitchen table eating Extra Spice oatmeal. *She would.*

"I need help deciding what to wear tonight, Cal." Darla put her nearly empty bowl in the sink without running water over the remaining contents that would soon stick. Beth stopped taking the noisemakers out of the bag.

"Darla, remember our rule. It gets rinsed before you get spinsed."

"Spinsed?" I asked.

"It's the word we made up for Darla so she can remember to wash her bowl before she gets fucked up. I want the house clean."

Beth was serious about this party. She reminded me of a mom, but since she was closer to my age, it seemed I was Cinderella helping my two stepsisters get ready for the ball. Thank god they weren't evil, fat women. I had dealt with two evil and fat foster sisters before. The ones that went to the *JFK* audition behind my back. It was comforting to know I had a new dress hanging in my closet that I could wear, courtesy of Beth. Maybe she *was* my fairy godmother.

Darla nodded to Beth's cleaning rule and we proceed upstairs. I sat on Darla's bed and watched her waif-like body slip into a dress. She took a look in the mirror. "I'm sick of this one. It doesn't look good on my thighs."

"How can anything look bad on you? You're a negative size."

"You keep it."

I looked down to see the true size. I wasn't far off. It was a zero. I would never get into it. Maybe goodwill would like it. *Hell,* I used to buy my clothes from there. I would love a dress like this. A few years ago, I might have been able to wear it, but I guess growth is what aging does. On second thought, it was the alcohol that promoted the growth.

"I can't fit into it, but thanks. You're so skinny."

"I might be skinny, but it levels out up here, you know." Darla patted her shoulders.

"What do you mean?"

"It's a whole weight up there, so it levels out the physical. I've tricked so many doctors into giving me prescriptions, I can see my permanent signature in the magnetic signature box at the Rite-Aid pharmacy."

It was the first time I heard Darla admit out loud that she knew she had a problem and that although she might look physically skinny, the drugs were mentally taking a toll.

"You know, if you aren't happy with your body, you could get plastic surgery." She suggested.

I was offended. "I'm a size two. I don't think I need that. I couldn't pay for it anyway."

"I'm not saying you do. I haven't seen you in a bathing suit. I'm just saying I advocate doing whatever makes a person happy."

Okay. So, if I want to rob a bank for money to make myself happy, then that would be okay? Just as long as I'm happy? Nice system of ethics. I mean, I know I wasn't innocent when it came to acquiring things in foster care, but that was different. I changed the subject, and I helped Darla decide on a red dress with a slit on the side.

"Who's coming to the party? Anyone from school?"

"Of course not. I mean, those kids can be okay, like, in class, but I prefer older, more sophisticated people. I have met a lot of people through Beth. There's this one guy coming named Peter that I like, and oh, he has a friend named Doug that you might like. They're both professionals."

Oh no. Not a set-up, I thought. I hated those. Ever since my friend Kim made me go out with a guy that told me how his mama had Parkinson's disease and when she got sick with the flu he had to give her a rectal thermometer because she would shake so much she'd bite down on the oral thermometer and crack the mercury, I swore off set-ups. They didn't have digital thermometers back then.

I wanted to see Jim again. Maybe he was adhering to the five-day rule. I thought he wouldn't care about waiting a certain number of days before calling, since he had already called Percy right after we met. The rules of dating were so stupid. Guys thought if they called too soon, they would look desperate.

I guessed some girls did tell their friends and say it was pathetic when guys called too soon, but I didn't think there should be a time limit. I thought they should only know it's psycho if they called more than once before you called them back. I wanted someone who defied the bullshit rules.

By 9 p.m. random strangers began to fill the house. I was definitely the youngest person in the house, and I felt a little out of place. The women sported fancy jewelry while the men looked polished like they came out of one of those J-Crew catalogue's I used to browse through when Jackson was finished with her monthly order.

I had on my new dress and looked just as nice, but I most certainly couldn't dress in expensive clothing every day. Although I realized this was New Years, I was sure most of these people dressed nice 24-7.

I would never fit into this world until I finished college and got a good job. It was different than when Jackson and people from school dressed up to go out. We just put on some tight tops and black pants and rolled out.

I poured my third glass of champagne when Beth entered the kitchen, insisting I meet her boyfriend, Kevin.

Shocked to see the guy with the green eyes and the funky birthmark on his cheek that I had thought was the owner's nephew and that Will told me was scum, I responded, "I've seen you before. At Black Sevens."

"Yeah, when was that?"

Kevin had a huge attitude, and I didn't think I'd said anything offensive. "A week ago." I responded, waiting for him to challenge.

Beth spoke instead. "Cal, you see so many people in there. You must have him confused with someone else."

I was positive I hadn't. And why would it be a big deal if I had seen him?

"Nice to meet you." Kevin said, stressing the, "meet."

I nodded. Beth was such a nice person that I couldn't see her with anyone like Kevin. Maybe opposites attracted, and she liked bad guys. She probably met him while stripping. Maybe Will was wrong about Kevin being scum, although I didn't get a warm feeling from him.

They left the kitchen and Darla entered with a man who she introduced as Peter. *Oh no.* The, "friend," was sure to be lurking somewhere. They said I should meet Doug, and they walked to the front room. I reluctantly followed.

They made the introductions, and I wanted to kill Darla. Doug was probably no more than thirty, but looked about fifty. Did she really think I would want to do *that?* And she was only twenty-two. What was with the daddy complex?

I tried to think of excuses to escape, but Darla instructed Doug to tell me what he did for a living. A financial planner. Well, that's nice. If I were ready to graduate and think about careers, then I would care. Maybe he would want to plan my financial future and tell me how to come up with a lot of money. Apparently, he was Darla's financial planner. Why did a twenty-two-year-old college student need a financial planner? I nodded politely to the small talk, but thought, *fuck, someone better get me outta here.* Then the very person who got me into the situation, offered an outlet for escape.

"Let's go to my room for refreshments."

I hadn't hit the bowl since Christmas and that was just what I needed. Then I could get away from big daddy by acting so stoned that I could wander away in a daze. I followed again as Peter kept high fiving the, "Dougmesiter." Were they really that excited to do drugs? Don't you have to stop at some age? And especially, feeling cool for doing them has got to get old.

I felt like I was about to go do drugs with my parents, or my two dads. I had them once in foster care. Two dads. That was interesting. It was the one time I went to a big city, Baton Rouge. Small towns and homos definitely don't mix. My two dads lasted a month until the dads broke up because one of them decided to switch sides.

Upstairs, Darla shut her door and went under her bed to a shoe box. She pulled out a bag of white powder and took a mirror and placed it on the floor. "I can borrow just a little from this."

What did she mean *borrow?* They weren't her drugs? She took out her University I.D. card with her picture and began chopping the cocaine into lines. It reminded me of the rare occasions when I cooked and chopped onions as fast as I could to avoid crying from the stench. But Darla had an intense look of pleasure on her face that suggested she could chop for hours.

Darla stopped spreading at 15 lines. *Hmm.* 8 ball. "I need 8. You guys can share the rest. Sorry, I'm selfish with my drugs."

I wanted to smack her. Darla's whole persona brought back images of Cracky Jacky. In addition to stripping and being a coke whore, Cracky Jacky was a street dealer that used her own product.

There's a rule on the street not to trust women. The only reason men trusted *her,* was because they knew they would get sex out of it. She thought it would be cute to bring along her *foster* daughter and make her part of the action. Cracky Jacky loved to surround herself with friends to snort with. There was always a party at our trailer.

Darla brought me back to reality by telling me it was my turn. "I don't do that shit." I got up and left the room. Let them talk about my insouciance. What the fuck did I care about making an impression with baldy? I didn't need to impress two over-aged frat boys masquerading as businessmen.

I headed back downstairs for more champagne. I finished another glass while I stood by the bottle, ready to pour more. Mmm. Maybe I would go to my room for a breather. I began to walk towards it, but got no further than the kitchen entrance when I banged into him, spilling champagne on his white shirt.

"Who knew the prettiest girl at the party would turn out to be the clumsiest?"

I looked up, surprised to see Jim smiling down at me, his white teeth in a perfect row. I hoped he was as great as his teeth, no braces required. "What're you doing here?"

"Friend of Beth Bloom. I was going to call you after the New Year. I've been caught up with work. That's why I'm so late tonight."

Where did he work at this time of night? Was he in healthcare? Did he work in a hospital? I led him back into the kitchen to wipe his shirt dry with a towel. I would have liked to wipe all of him dry. I picked up a bottle of champagne. Sometimes, I just didn't know when to stop. Maybe I was no better than Darla. After all, like the Dean told us at freshman orientation, "alcohol is a drug." In my new world it was the most benign.

I poured Jim some champagne. "This will help you forget work." I was tipsy and couldn't believe I had just said something so generic. Hopefully, he didn't think I was as dull as old baldy upstairs. I took Jim's hand and led him to any empty sofa in the front room that must have been the parlor long ago.

"I can't believe I went from getting a false number to sitting on your couch."

I took him literally. "Nothing's mine here. Not even the futon I sleep on."

"A futon, huh? That's the most advantageous piece of furniture."

"Wise guy." I joked and playfully gave him a push on his shoulder, feeling the champagne ease my normal barrier.

"Hippy, bohemian lifestyles are cool." Jim continued.

"I have no money. I was a child of the system. A ward of the state. You have no idea what it feels like to be imprisoned by an institution."

"I do. I'm a Coasty."

"A what e?"

"A Coasty. I'm in the Coastguard."

I thought how I shouldn't assume people don't know what things are like until I get to know them. No wonder he wasn't like the suits surrounding us. Although he was groomed just as well, if not better with his good posture and manners. The only difference was his cropped, short hair. And I heard military type guys loved to spend their money out drinking. That might explain why he tipped me so much. But still, his job couldn't be as stifling as my ownership by the state.

My nature was to challenge. "Well, I had a peripatetic childhood."

"A what?"

"I lived all over Louisiana. Abita Springs….."

"Good beer."

"And water." I continued, "Angola, Bayou Vista, Chalmette, Houma, Harahan, Lafitte, Lake Charles, New Iberia. I think you get the point."

"Small towns, but we still have city hopping in common. I've travelled with my job."

"So the Coast Guard. Maybe one day you can take me out on your boat. I've never been out on a big boat before. Only little fishing boats in the bayou." I was testing him, trying to see if he might have long term potential or whether he just wanted a hook-up.

"Well, I'm not that exciting. I'm a yeoman. I work behind the scenes in the office doing boring administrative type stuff. Paper work. Do you want some more champagne? It's almost midnight. Your glass has to be full."

I nodded and went to stand but was unstable. Jim's hands grabbed my waist and held me from falling face first into the couch. Yo, man! If his hands felt this nice against my body, I couldn't wait to know how the rest of him felt. He stood and we headed to the kitchen to fill our plastic champagne flutes for the final time that evening.

Beth and Kevin stood by the sink kissing. Kevin stood out from the rest of the people at the party. I wasn't sure what she saw in him. He dressed like he thought he was a rock star. While everyone else was dressed up in nice pants and cocktail dresses, he thought he could be the exception. He must not give a shit. Seemed rude to me when his girlfriend was throwing the party and had picked the dress code.

He also had a, "too cool," air about him because his nose stayed in the air like he was sticking his fingers up it like a three-year-old. He seemed edgy because his hands shook a little. I was afraid saying the wrong thing to him like I had earlier would piss him off and send him into a tirade.

"Time to play DJ." Beth said and literally skipped to the radio. I smiled at her carefree, drunken behavior.

I poured more champagne. Jim told me he had to talk to Kevin for a minute and he would come find me. *He was a friend of this creep?* I followed slowly. I was really curious about what they had to say to one another. I used to stealthily listen to parents in foster care. It was nice to have some warning before I moved to a new home.

I heard Kevin tell Jim, "your fingers are supposed to be on the pulse of the sector. You have access to information. Use it faster."

"Very soon there will be plenty of fish coming in. Call it high season."

Although I knew I hadn't learned everything about Jim in one coffee sitting, he hadn't mentioned to me that he enjoyed fishing, even when I mentioned fishing in the bayou. Maybe he would take *me* out fishing sometime, my drunk self thought.

"I need a bigger supply. Paul will be angry." Kevin said. I wondered if he was a liquor distributor, but what would *that* have to do with fish?

"Let's leave here soon and discuss further." Jim suggested.

"Sure. Beth will be pissed I'm not staying over. I'll have to listen to her bitch."

How loving, I thought. Great. These two were just waiting to go out and party after this party? I guessed Jim didn't want to stay on the futon after all. That sucked. I thought he really liked me. Maybe he was playing games and fish meant women.

Jim turned away from Kevin and saw me standing there. I took off. It was a few minutes before midnight and Beth blasted Prince's *1999* on the stereo. Darla hadn't come downstairs with the boys. They were probably double teaming her. Good. At least I was off the hook, but maybe the Dougmesiter was my only option. Gross. I figured I would end up alone if he was.

I moved around the excited party guests and found a spot to stand. At 11:59 everyone began the countdown. 5,4,3,2,1. Happy New Year. It was 1999. I downed more champagne as streamers hit me in the face and noisemakers irritated my ears.

"Wow, you can out drink me. You're hard to catch." Jim tapped my glass with his.

"Maybe you should stick to fish. I don't fall for bait."

"Oh, back there?" He pointed to the spot where he and Kevin had their fishy conversation. "My hobby is fishing. Kevin knows real fisherman that will sell what I catch. Just trying to make an honest buck on the side doing something I enjoy."

"You have intel for fishing?"

"I know when top fisherman go out and where they will be so I don't tread on their territory. Kevin gets uptight about things since he knows those guys." Jim whispered, "If you haven't noticed, he's a little unbalanced." I smiled. He had a way of reassuring me. Still, what did Paul, the owner of Black Sevens have to do with this? If a Bourbon street bar owner was involved, I thought fish might be a metaphor for whores.

I nodded, still not sure to trust him. He took my hand and led me to the front door. He kissed me under the mistletoe left up from Christmas. It felt more like a passionate kiss rather than a courtesy kiss goodnight and because of its long duration and passion, I thought maybe he did like me.

"I'm sorry, I have to leave." My paranoia kicked in. Was our meeting destined to last forever because of the romanticism of mistletoe? Or was it doomed because mistletoe is also a parasite that absorbs water and nutrients from its host tree? Nothing in my life lasted very long, and I hoped this would be different.

I watched him get into his BMW. *Nice car on a Coast Guard salary*, I thought. Maybe he was one of those people with family money that just did their job to be noble? Or maybe he didn't mind high car payments.

He rolled down his window. "You're trouble, aren't you? Listening to that conversation earlier." He should know I listen to protect myself. "Just watching my back." I smiled.

When I turned back to head inside, Doug was staring at me. I shrugged and headed away from him up the stairs. I was finished with the party until Beth needed help cleaning up. My night was complete. It was my New Year. The decisions were all mine, and I was glad the Dougmeister was *not* my only option.

Chapter 8

All night long after the party, I dreamed of that kiss with Jim. For the first time, I felt like I had met someone who might be worth keeping around. He didn't take long to win me over when he called two days later, as he said he would.

For our first date, Jim took me over to the Audubon Zoo. We could walk from my street. I had never been to a zoo before. In fact, I was afraid of animals. In small towns, everyone chained their big dogs. I was scared of them because they always drooled all over the place and barked at you like you were a piece of fresh meat. Kind of like how the college boys looked at the new freshman girls every year.

The first animals we saw at the Zoo were lions. When we went near them, I was reluctant to walk up close. Jim took my hand and led me towards them, and I still flinched.

"What's wrong with you?"

I explained my past with animals.

"You should have told me. We didn't have to come here."

"No, it's cool."

"Let's leave."

"No, I'm enjoying it. After all, they *are* behind cages."

"Guess you won't be watching Animal Planet with me."

I smiled and excused myself to use the restroom. When I came out from around the corner, Jim jumped out and scared me half to death. He handed me the stuffed lion. "Trying to get you to conquer your fear. Thought I'd start with one that won't drool. And look at the smile across his face. He's a friendly lion."

"I can keep this?" I slipped thinking of my time with Cracky Jacky. I explained that my wonderful foster mother would put drugs where no one suspected in the early days: my teddy bear. I would hold the bear in the Waffle House, but then leave without him. I would cry at parting with another stuffed animal.

Gus, Cuddles, BooBoo, BearBear, the list goes on. Cracky Jacky would say, "Stop crying or I'm gonna give you back like them dresses I git where I tuck in the tag so I can return em. Look, think of em like they're a foster kid too. They gotta move to a new home."

"That's awful." Jim responded to my story.

Jim had southern charm, opening doors for me and insisting on paying for everything, unlike the small town boys that tried to get me to pay for their cigarettes. At least I was contributing to their demise. I'm really not that cold hearted. I'm just not into the wife beater type.

When I was little, well, really until my grades dropped, I wanted to be a doctor. I thought that this way when I was sick, I would always be able to take care of myself. As I grew older, all the girls my age tried to attract boys to take care of them. But when Billy Bob and Cyrus Ray only aspired to be clerks at the Five and Dime, I knew I would have to fend for myself. The last thing I aspired to be was some fat housewife on welfare whose only purpose was to pop out more babies.

After the zoo, Jim walked me back home and we kissed on the front porch. That evening the crickets seemed louder than normal. Maybe they were just coming out or maybe my senses were heightened.

***

Jim picked me up at the house the following night for our second date. He told me he had a present for me. I was very surprised when he handed me a CD. He had already given me the stuffed animal. "I know you said the other day that you loved the Beastie Boys, so I got you their new CD."

"This has my new favorite song, Intergalactic. Thank you so much." I kissed him on the cheek and he held my hand as we drove. I melted and got all self-conscious. I knew CDs weren't an indication of a lasting romance, and I tried not to plan our future.

I stared down at my new dress. Jim had told me on the phone to wear something cute and nice because we were going to a fancy place to eat. He had already seen me in the black cocktail dress, so I decided to buy another new item of clothing. I still had to run that errand for Beth to pay for the New Years dress and jeans, since I used my work money from the days after New Years on more clothes. I would start saving soon.

We pulled up to Julia Street in the Warehouse District and the valet opened my door. Aside from Jackson taking me to a nice restaurant for my birthday last year, this was a first. I felt like a princess. Guess it didn't take too much.

Jim grabbed my hand as we walked into Emeril's Restaurant. Man was it high class. The décor alone was fancy, I couldn't wait to taste the food. We sat down at a table in the middle of the restaurant and opened our menus. I began to peruse as Jim picked up another menu full of just wine.

"We'll have the Shafer Cabernet." I nodded and took the wine menu from him to see for myself what that meant. A red. Sixty-five bucks a bottle. *Shit. That's mega expensive.* I suggested something called a Hillside Select to save him money, but he told me not to worry about the cost.

I ordered the weirdest assortment of food I had ever tasted, like a cheesecake that wasn't dessert, but an appetizer with crabmeat and a salmon stuffed with corn. Jim insisted we order a chocolate soufflé made with something called Grand Marnier for dessert that you had to order upfront because of prep time. This was certainly no fast food restaurant. I marveled at the high-class scene around me, versus my normal college scene.

The wine guy came to pour Jim's choice. He called himself a wine steward. I thought those people were only on airplanes. He uncorked the wine and poured just a little swallow for Jim to try. Then he poured mine and left us to toast after Jim nodded his head at the little sip he sampled.

"To meeting the prettiest girl in The Big Easy." Jim raised his glass to mine.

I blushed and clinked my glass against his. When I returned it to the table, it landed on my fork that flew off the table and onto the floor. *Nice move, Calina.* I went to pick it up. I felt like Julia Roberts in *Pretty Woman* minus the prostitute part. For me the film would have to be named *Clumsy Woman*.

Jim stopped me from reaching over to pick up the fork. "They'll get it and bring you a fresh one."

"Sorry. I'm clumsy. And I guess I'm nervous. I've never been to a place this nice before."

"Relax. You don't have to worry with me. I wasn't raised in opulence with fancy meals. My dad was New Orleans heat and my mom was a housewife."

"Mine was too. Killed in the line of duty."

"We'll save my family story for another time. I don't want to ruin our night." Jim told me.

At the end of the meal, my stomach swelled and provided the substantial evidence that I had eaten a full course meal. It felt sinful to eat food that good when some people didn't even have a piece of bread. I thought I had eaten more in one sitting than I ever had in my entire life and that Jim would think I was a pig eating all of that food. But he said it was awesome to see a girl eat all that I did. Apparently, the only girls he must have been dating were strippers down from Black Sevens at Dick's Palace. On second thought, *they* came in all shapes and sizes.

He asked if I minded going out after dinner. Beth and Kevin wanted to meet up somewhere, and Jim had suggested an art gallery. Apparently, he loved art.

"As much as fishing?"

"Much better than fishing. Fishing can be dirty. This is elegant and intellectual."

***

When we entered the art gallery for a new artists' display, we looked around for Kevin and Beth. Jim told me that Kevin operated on his own time. Once again, my impression of Kevin was *not* a positive one.

Jim led me down a hallway of paintings done in a plethora of styles. We stood in front of one painting that looked like those 3-D posters that everyone went crazy over when I was a kid. I could never see the image everyone else seemed to see. They were like a page out of a magazine called *Highlights* for children that I loved to get my hands on to find the missing objects.

Jim told me this painting was done in a style called Pointillism. As we went down the isle, Jim claimed to see many things I didn't, although I thought it was cute how he incessantly explained the art to me. He had an interest a long time ago and began reading art books.

Kevin and Beth finally showed, but Kevin said he didn't want to stay. His arms shook.

"You chose a place that is so public."

"Well, since you want dark and secluded, what's your idea?" Jim asked.

"Red Room." Beth chirped.

A bar didn't seem very private, but we all exited the gallery for the new destination. At least Jim and I got to see some good art before Kevin rudely tore us away. In the car, I asked, "What's wrong with him? His manners are nonexistent."

"He means well." I didn't want to bash on my new guy's friend, so I kept quiet.

A few minutes later, we entered the Red Room, an all red carpeted and red walled posh restaurant and bar. People in jeans were turned away at the door.

Although Jackson could get us in anywhere, we usually stuck to bars close to school like Tom Collins, a dark, smoke filled hole where all the waitresses spent their time before, during and after work, doing coke with the owner's son.

Here, all the patrons were on coke. Beth took me with her to the bathroom while Kevin and Jim waited for a table.

In the bathroom, Beth pulled me inside a stall with her. She laid out a line of cocaine on the square inch of the toilet paper dispenser. Snort. "I only do it sometimes when I dance to put me in a better mood, but Kevin's getting on my nerves tonight. Want some?"

"No thanks. You don't need another addict roommate."

"Harsh, but true."

"Why is Kevin bugging you?" I asked, as she squatted over the toilet to relieve herself. If I thought I *wasn't* going to be close with my new roommates, I was wrong as my knees almost touched her crotch as I became one with the stall door. We should have used the handicap stall.

"You know, boyfriend stuff. Not giving me enough attention. He's obsessed with money. Speaking of, I still need you to run that errand for me."

"Sure, anytime. Just find me when I'm not working."

We joined the guys a minute later at a corner table. "Paul said to hunt it down like a dog looking for a treat cause it's what puts the food in your sorry mouth."

Whoa. As soon as I was with Jim for a longer period of time, this guy was going to have to take a hike. Why would Jim even let him talk to him like that?

Beth ordered. "We'll have two bottles of the 88 Dom Perignon please."

"Whatever that is, we don't have it at Black Sevens."

Beth laughed. "It's a very fine champagne."

I looked at Jim who winked at me.

Kevin waved a hundred dollar bill at the waitress. "Kevin, you know Chris said your money is no good here." The waitress, Vanessa, according to her tiny name tag, told him.

"It's for your tip, darlin."

Despite feeling like I was living the good life going to fancy places and having guys provide me with essentials off of Maslow's Hierarchy of needs first stage, Kevin freaked me out. I decided to get to the bottom of him, not knowing the bottom wasn't attainable at this time.

"Are you a liquor distributor?" I asked Kevin.

"What gave you that stupid idea?"

Well, dumb ass, maybe from the fact that you were talking about the owner of Black Sevens, get drinks for free at bars and always seem to know their owners, I thought.

"We're gonna go dance." Beth grabbed me and took me out on the dance floor.

"What's your boyfriend's problem?" I asked as she gyrated around me. *Damn, strippers can really move.*

"He just doesn't like questions."

"I didn't know inquiring about his job would make him mad."

"Don't be offended. Family money. Spoiled." She said as she sniffed loudly.

***

An hour later, Jim took me home. By that point, I didn't look at Kevin and had had four vodka cranberries and two vodka shots just to avoid being annoyed. I didn't want to let my wasted self screw up with Jim. I wanted him to last. He was already so thoughtful and generous and I wanted things to stay that way.

As he pulled up to my house, I told him, "I had a great time." We began to make out.

"When can I see you again?"

Wow. He was being a total gentleman by not trying to make a move to come upstairs. Or, if that *was* his move, it was pretty benign.

"Well, I'm working the next few nights." I responded.

"Call me when you're free."

Jim leaned over and kissed me again. He was such a passionate kisser. Maybe I just really liked him and actually felt more than wet tongues. Hallelujah. Praise the Lord.

Chapter 9

Three nights later, I was on my third consecutive night shift and all I could think about was Jim. Will asked, "who you wastin all that attention on?"

Although Will was the nicest manager, he was friendlier to me than to the other girls. Maybe he realized I was book smart as well as street smart, and he found this appealing. I found him more interesting to talk to than my co-workers. For one thing, we were competing against one another all night to see who could sell more shots. The conversations ended up being manipulative distractions.

My other distaste for my co-waitresses was the fact that they reminded me too much of the small town girls and the mentality that I had escaped. They probably thought that I thought I was too good for them.

Round Randy buzzed Will on the walkie-talkie. "Did Paul say to do the cover charge tonight?" His voice screeched.

"It's Friday night. He don't have to tell us on the nights we pull in big numbers. It's a given. Enter three hundred people at ten dollars each."

I shot Will a confused look. I had never seen the club initiate a cover charge. "I didn't know you were clairvoyant, Will."

"What're you talking about?"

"If we're gonna do a cover charge, how do you know how many people will walk through those doors the rest of the night?"

He laughed, and I wasn't sure if it was at me.

"Nevermind what you hear us talk about. We're just discussing business."

How could a miscalculated cover charge be business?

"Hey darlin." Jim twirled me around and kissed me on the lips. Had I not heard his voice, I might have decked him he gave me such a surprise.

"The truth comes out. I saw her thinking about you earlier." Will winked.

"No more PDA. I have to pretend I'm single for better tips. Only eyes for my customers."

"What's PDA?" Jim asked.

Will looked at him incredulously. "Well, I didn't think eight years was a generational gap. There's no excuse for him."

Will was up on pop culture lingo only because of twenty-year old Jessica.

"It's public display of affection." I informed my clueless, new male friend.

"You two together or sumthin?" Will asked.

I blushed. What were we? Dating? How did one answer that? What did together mean? Let Jim take this one. I'm not going there.

"She's my girl, so make sure no one messes with her." He smiled at me. I stood emotionless, thinking the label was fast, but inside all my organs were smiling their own shit-eating grin. Although it was just a label, it made me feel important.

"Don't let us keep you from selling your shots." Jim said.

An hour later, I turned in my last empty tray and went downstairs to find Jim. I grabbed his waist from behind, and he turned around. I kissed him. "Now all my customers know they've been had."

We left the club, and I noticed the bouncers had still not initiated a cover charge. Outside, the bible preacher with the giant cross was in full force. He began to follow us. "Give God your pledge of celibacy. Do not sin in the eyes of God. He is all knowing."

If I had been drunk, I would have challenged the preacher that if he were female, he would have a hard time being celibate around Jim. Hell, males would too. Jim put his arms around me and hugged me. He looked toward the bible preacher to give him a cold stare.

"I don't like people trying to enforce their views on someone else."

More cool points. When we arrived back at my house, I opened my bedroom door to find a desk sitting in my room.

"I think someone made a mistake. This must be for Darla or Beth. They love to buy new things."

He grabbed my arm before I could leave the room to find my roommates. "Wait, it's for you."

"Huh?"

"I got it for you for school."

Triple quadruple cool points. His thoughtfulness made me want him more. Not to mention, I liked being spoiled since I rarely had been before. I hugged him and wanted to freeze him at that moment and never let him go away. Possessive or not, I didn't care. I kissed him.

"I always wanted to go to school, but there was no money for me."

I remembered reality, and I awkwardly turned away. "I won't be in school for a little while." I was so embarrassed. I didn't know him that well. He might think I was a dumb ass for losing my scholarship money.

Jim faced me. "I thought you started back up."

"Everyone but me. That's why I'm working at the club. I need money to go back." I explained further. I had called the financial aid office as soon as they opened after the first of the year. A loan would not come through in time for the new semester.

"Calina, you're the smartest girl I've ever met."

"That might not say a lot." I teased.

"No, really. When I see something I want, I go after it. I see that in you. You're taking the initiative. That's hot."

I just wanted to sleep with this guy. And I did.

***

The next morning I woke before Jim and stared at his face, tracing it with my index finger. Forehead, right cheek, lips, nose, left cheek. I ended at his neck. I love to look at people with their eyes closed. They look so innocent and helpless when only their subconscious is working. Staring at Jim, I hoped he would last.

At that moment, I realized that in the past, I subconsciously picked guys I knew wouldn't last for some reason, usually emotional unavailability, because I didn't want to go through losing anyone.

Jim opened his eyes when he felt my hand on his chest near his heart. He smiled and gave me a familiar glance. At least he didn't forget where he was. "Time for round three, he asked?" At least he hadn't forgotten what happened the night before either.

We had first done it on the futon and then decided to christen the desk. He left a few hours and two more long rounds later. Man, did he have stamina.

After he left, I could still smell his scent on my body, but it wasn't enough. That could be re-created with some cologne and sweat. But his body and physical presence, his face, could never be emulated. I was already getting attached, something I didn't normally do. I was still smiling in bed when Beth knocked on the door.

"Come in."

"Cal, I need you to run the errand you said you'd do to pay for the jeans."

I nodded and stretched my arms.

"You had a good night. You're glowing. Welcome to the family."

"What do you mean?"

"You know, Jim's friends with Kev." I still didn't understand that, but I wasn't going to be a controlling girl and tell him who he could and could *not* hang out with.

"Back to business. It's going to be a tough semester for me, so I have more if you want to make even more money to add to your work money. You'll really grow that savings account."

That's what I liked to hear. "What exactly is this errand?"

"Just dropping off some goods to people. I wrote down the address. Nothing you have to be concerned about. The only thing you have to do is drop off a package and receive an envelope with cash. When you receive the envelope and you aren't going straight home, just take the money out and put it in your sneaker. You'll meet a guy named Lidell. He's from Slidell. I told him you were coming."

Sounded easy enough. But weird too.

***

A few hours later, I left. I had to be at work that night at eight p.m., so I decided to do the errand on the way. Four nights in a row in the bar was getting old. I was exhausted and my mouth hurt from smiling and giving the catch phrase, "wanna shot?" I looked at the address. Somewhere in the Garden District.

I sat on the streetcar with my book bag. Inside, was the package Beth had given me, a shoebox labeled Manolo Blahniks. Beth spent more money on shoes than anyone I ever knew. For stripping acts, I presumed. I felt the shoebox and it seemed a little heavy for shoes. Enquiring minds wanted to know.

In foster care, I had a mom who loved to read all of those trashy magazines like *The Enquirer* and *Star*. I would read them after she was done only to pretend I was one of the famous people with problems rather than poor with problems.

The street car wized through the garden district where all the mansions stood with their wrought iron gates and trees with Spanish moss slightly blowing in the winter night. What business could Beth possibly have with these rich people? She didn't tell me she was a personal assistant.

And, if Lidell really was from Slidell, I didn't think Slidell was full of rich people.

I zipped open the book bag. The outside of the shoebox had loose masking tape around it. Easy enough to take off and put right back on. Shouldn't I know exactly how I was paying Beth back for those designer jeans?

I opened the shoebox to find a canister of tennis balls instead of high heels. *What the hell?* Delivering tennis balls certainly wasn't an equal exchange for designer jeans. I popped the top and touched a ball.

In high school gym class, we used to have to play tennis. All of us girls tried to copy that *Clueless* movie and say we had nose jobs that prevented us from playing, but no one in small town Louisiana can afford something like that. We were just plain lazy and wanted to stare at the boys, not let them see our athletic abilities or lack thereof. Our noses were all good anyway. Never underestimate a small town girl. Some of the prettiest girls and models come out of small towns. *And the smartest.*

I rotated the ball in my hand with the shelter of my book bag. Peaking in, I saw a slit on one side. I turned to look at the person next to me. He was an older man staring straight ahead. He probably had weak eyes.

I slightly opened the slit and fingered a small bag that held what looked like sugar. Don't panic, I told myself. As soon as I'm on the streets, I'll figure it out.

On Washington Avenue and St. Charles, I got off and walked towards Prytania street. A chill went through my body as I faced the destination for my errand at a City of The Dead, eerie Lafayette Cemetery number 1 established in 1833. I knew the film *Interview with a Vampire* had made this cemetery famous, and I was finally face to face with it. Although Anne Rice romanticized it, I found nothing redeemable about death.

I ducked inside the gates. In New Orleans the dead are buried in tombs above ground because much of the city is below sea level. If graves were not above ground and it flooded, they would rise and the bodies would pop out like in the pool scene from the movie *Poltergeist*. Lord, I watched too many movies before college.

Too bad it wasn't a holiday. Then I would have some light. During Holidays, family members leave votive candles, lining the sun-bleached tombs. The candles cast shadows in the night to honor the departed and to remind them they still have living relatives that care.

I remembered that the cemetery is supposedly home to a mass burial sight of yellow fever epidemic victims in 1853. Not a place I wanted to be at night. I shook off a chill. I looked around and only saw some freaks dressed as Vampires. Then again, maybe they were real live ones.

I opened the book bag and pulled out a tennis ball. I opened the small Ziploc bag inside and put a finger in. I tasted the white powder and my tongue turned numb. Definitely *not* sugar. Shit, there must be at least three ounces of cocaine. I quickly calculated in my head. At roughly sixty dollars a gram and twenty-eight grams equaling one ounce, I would be correct if I received approximately five thousand dollars.

Not that stripping was bad money, but this might explain the Visa Black Card?

Fuck, what has Beth gotten herself into selling drugs? Wait, what have I gotten myself into carrying them? Shoe box my ass. If I got caught, then what would become of me? A school drop out, drug runner? I'd return to small town Louisiana and become the white trash I tried to avoid. No way.

All of a sudden someone grabbed me from behind and spun me around. I stood facing a large black man with gold chains around his neck, a giant L in the middle. Too bad I left my Master P CD back home. Now I wouldn't be able to fit in and prove I liked rap too.

"You here for Celexa?"

"Um, yeah."

"What's the p-word?"

"Password?"

"Yeah."

"She didn't tell me I'd needed one."

"I'm just playin. Name's Lidell from Slidell. Got any good Jazz in that backpack?"

I had stereotyped him with rap. Who would have known he enjoyed the music of the city. "Sorry, left my CDs at home."

He placed his hands out for the goods.

"The envelope please." I said. Coming up on the street, you learn to get yours upfront. Whatever it may be. You better believe Lidell from Slidell was gonna give me the money first.

"What you think this is? An awards show?" He asked. I had always wondered if they had TVs in the ghetto.

"Funny. I think they read teleprompters these days. Eliminates the suspense if you ask me."

"You a smart ass. Here." Lidell from Slidell handed me the envelope, and I bent over to slip off my shoe. I took the money out of the envelope.

Beth hadn't given me any instructions to count the money, but I began. Wasn't she worried this thug would stiff her?

I began to count hundreds. Hundreds turned to thousands! 5000. Glad to know my calculations from my time with Cracky Jacky were still accurate.

"You ain't gotta count it. There's trust." Apparently, Beth was a *longtime* drug dealer. My curiosity kept growing.

I handed the shoebox over to Lidell from Slidell who took the drugs out and placed them underneath his shorts. "The po-lice don't look there."

Well it was a good thing he *wasn't* placing them in his pants to be a pervert. But I knew better.

Foster Mom Cracky Jacky became *Wacky* Cracky Jacky when she decided to diss the teddy bear plot and instead, put the drugs in *my* panties. She would point to my crouch, "Ain't no cop gonna risk a molestation charge by pulling down there. Specially on a lil girl."

Once at home, Wacky Cracky Jacky thought her idea of teaching me math was dividing quantities. Maybe that's why I was decent in math at an early age, so at least she furthered my education. She explained the white stuff would bring us great riches and more teddy bears as she mixed the drugs with B-12 powder and told me she was making the original stuff healthy by putting in the additive vitamin. She didn't look too healthy herself after she snorted like a pig. In fact, I thought she looked like she needed a doctor one time when she convulsed on the floor. I didn't know there was such a thing as 9-1-1 at the time so instead, I called the pediatrician.

There's a rule on the street-never use your own product. Wacky Cracky Jacky went to jail. I went to a new home, narrowly avoiding "juvie," juvenile detention, because they caught us when I tripped and the drugs fell out of my pants. They then checked my teddy bear and found more drugs there. I told them I wasn't that smart or stupid to do these things and they released me.

The police might not check a woman because men on the street don't trust women to deal, however, they might check a man. I felt compelled to warn Lidell. "The 5-0 *do* look there on men, Lidell."

"How you know this?"

"Foster care."

"Now that's some fucked up shit, girl."

"How long have you known Beth?"

Lidell from Slidell looked like he was taking a shit, his forehead muscles contracted he was concentrating so hard.

"More like how long she known Lidell from Slidell."

Nothing like a little ego from the ghetto. The money filling the bottom of my shoe, I said, "later," and headed for the streetcar, marveling that the amount of cash just raised my sixty dollar black Reeboks to 5060 dollar sneakers. I felt like an NBA superstar with specially designed shoes.

But, what had I done? Those old crack hos back in Baton Rouge thought they were big time. Ha. No more Calina Lefevre. Get a load of Calina Crackfevre.

Chapter 10

All during work, I stressed. Although the five thousand was buried deep in my new and improved sneakers, I felt I was transparent and people would know I had just been on a drug run. Beth worked that night and would get home after me. You bet I waited up for her.

She walked into the house with her high heels hitting the hardwood. I informed her I needed to talk.

"Can't it wait til morning? I had one too many private dances on the second floor tonight." The second floor was the dark area where *anything* could happen.

"You mean you *don't* want your *five thousand* dollars?"

"I trust you to hold onto it til morning." I couldn't wait and went into a tirade starting with my visit with Lidell from Slidell.

"Don't go getting all sanctimonious on me, Calina. It's no worse than what I do stripping or what you do cocktailing for the club. People pay for a service."

"They pay for alcohol, not illegal drugs."

"The club waters down those shots. They barely pay for anything but your cute face to serve them. The drug money I make is no worse than the money you make hustling people."

"You're fucked up. That's a lot different. You should have told me what I was doing. If I had been caught on that streetcar or the street, I'd have ended up in jail. And if it's the same as juvie, then I don't want to be there." Although I had spent a short time in juvenile hall twice, these misunderstandings were enough.

"But you wouldn't have gotten caught. No one suspects it from chicks. On the street, men don't trust females. The cops don't expect females to have drugs, especially ones that look as innocent as you, and they don't want to search women for fear of sexual harassment charges. It just so happens that Celexa has an, "in," on the street and a reputation to uphold."

"Well, you can uphold it without me. My debt with you is settled. I don't want to end up back where I came from. I know about the females and pants thing, and I was caught as a child and put in juvie until they realized my foster Mom was the culprit, not an eight-year-old."

"This is big time, Calina. Not some po dunk town. And don't think I met you out of coincidence. Yes, I was at the library because I had to be, but I watched you, waiting for the right time to meet you and get you out of that slave wage job."

"What?"

"I knew you were from a small town. You have that tough edge to you, even though you look corn fed. I looked into your background."

"You're fucked up."

"A little. But I'm trying to help you a lot more than those horrible foster homes ever did. I know you can use the money, Cal. You'd be one of Celexa's girls. No taking your clothes off or prostituting yourself. It's not degrading. Think about it. It's two to three hundred a delivery, depending on the amount."

"You still strip so how is this the answer?"

"I like to dance."

I wouldn't win this conversation. She did what she did, and I wouldn't turn her to the honest side. In fact, I felt the dark side coming a little too close with its easy money.

I left Beth's room mad as hell. How dare she try to ruin my life and make me a drug runner. I appreciated that she wanted to help someone she hardly knew, but Bourbon Street was one thing, running cocaine, another.

I slammed my bedroom door. I didn't want to talk to my wacky roommates ever again. No wonder Darla was such an addict. She was running too, using her own product that she pulled out at the party. I wasn't sure how she hadn't been caught yet and in jail like the fate of foster mom Wacky Cracky Jacky.

I laid on the futon and stared around the sparse room. It did look like a real room with Beth's help, even if it was minimalist style. Now, it made sense that she mentioned maybe I could have a car soon. No. I could never help distribute drugs.

All my life I had to be the parent and make decisions. I was a quick thinker and sometimes impulsive, but I always had a plan. I needed a retreat, an outlet, a safe haven where I wouldn't think about drugs. I dialed Jim's pager number. *Yes, we still had pagers back then.* I hoped he was still awake.

***

An hour later, Jim pulled up in front of the house. I took my seat in this BMW and he leaned over and kissed me. We drove down Saint Charles Avenue hand in hand until we entered the Warehouse District before the French Quarter.

"Sorry to reach out at four in the morning."

"No problem. I was up. Went fishing and I couldn't sleep."

"Catch anything?"

"Just some bottom feeders."

When I didn't see Jim in the club that night, I was worried he was at some other bar hitting on chicks. The beginning stages of relationships made me paranoid.

"Aren't you exhausted from work?" He asked.

I told Jim I felt edgy in the house and that Darla and Beth were up being loud. It was my first lie, but I wasn't about to divulge the details of my fight with Beth.

After parking the car underground, we took an elevator up to the top floor. Jim opened his apartment door for me.

"Lady first."

I dropped my bag on the floor by his sofa and took a look around. The ceilings were high like in my house. I estimated fifteen feet.

"You live alone?"

"One bedroom." Jim told me as he pulled me towards it.

"Wait, I want to see all your stuff. This apartment is so nice. Well decorated for a guy."

"It's just stuff, Calina. It doesn't mean anything."

It did to me. It meant he was self-sufficient. "I know, but you did a great job decorating. Even with the blinds." They matched his couch.

"I hired a decorator."

A photograph of a woman holding two little boys and a man standing behind them caught my eye. I lifted it to examine it closer. "Is this your family?"

"Was. Until I was thirteen."

"I'm sorry."

"See, I'm an orphan like you. We have a lot in common."

"What happened?"

"A major drug gang he was investigating had him killed. My mother and brother were with him in the car when he was gunned down."

"Wow. I'm so sorry."

"Don't be. It's over. The real mistake my father made was leaving guardianship to my uncle."

Jim moved to the stereo and pushed play on the CD player. Nina Simone began to sing, "I put a spell on you."

I sat on the couch as Jim moved to the kitchen and asked, "Red or white tonight?"

"In the morning, I prefer white, please." I said as I opened the blinds a touch to reveal the light of the early morning horizon.

He handed me my white wine. "Maybe one day we'll each get the family we deserve." I was careful not to say, "our," family. I didn't want to freak him out by insinuating we would have a family together, but at that moment, I felt very connected to him. I had no idea he hadn't had a family for so long like me.

"We will." He kissed me and threw me over his shoulders. "But for now, we can go practice for the future."

I feel asleep an hour later, realizing the aroma normally left by freshly caught fish, was missing.

I woke at noon, feeling the effects of staying up all night. The nightlife really wore out my body. I hadn't even thought about my prior drug running activity and how Beth invited me into *that* family. *Hmm. Family.* That was a new thought. Having a bond with people that no one could take away.

Stop. I couldn't think like that. I don't want a negative bond. My mind pictured me as a positively charged ion bonding with a negative, and the only thing that could result would be negative. I felt guilty thinking about illegal drug activity when Jim's family had died from it.

I turned over to curl up next to him, but all I found were white sheets. He couldn't be walking out on me in his own place. Maybe he was in the next room.

I walked to the kitchen and found a note. It read, "Cal, I forgot I had to be at the office early today. See you soon. I left you money to take a cab home. Jim." Jim left the number of a cab driver at the bottom of his brief note.

The cab driver picked me up ten minutes later. "Name's George." George had a slight accent and I deduced he was Mexican.

"Nice to meet you. I'm Cal."

"So Cal, hey, that's funny. I used to live in the other L.A. Get it? SoCal, Southern California."

I wished I was there right now. With my wine headache, it would be better than listening to him babble.

"Give Jim a message for me, will ya?"

Not that most cab drivers didn't try to give out their business cards in hopes of repeat customers, but Jim had really made friends in New Orleans.

"Sure."

"Tell him I want two girl next time I see him, okay?"

"Huh?"

"You know, whatever medium size is. Not too big."

"Are you kidding me?"

"How long you been together?"

"I met him a few weeks ago."

He nodded and left me curious. What a sleaze. "How does he find you girls? Connections at one of the strip clubs?"

"Nevermind. Not important. I'll talk to him soon. Nothin' to worry bout darlin."

Too late. The fact that the guy I was seeing got girls for other men had to make me wonder about his activities. Was he a pimp? He certainly didn't fit the stereotypical profile of the ones I knew of in small towns.

What if I *wasn't* the only girl he was sleeping with? And we had had such an amazing night. When I got out of the car, my face turned red, and I felt like puking. Why would he buy me a desk and seem so sweet? How many other girls was he buying gifts for? Sure, he was out fishing last night.

I could only count on myself in life. I knew that, but at that moment, I was more vulnerable than ever. To make matters worse, I opened my mail. The U.S. government wanted to inform me that I would need to start paying back my loans in 6 months if I was not back in school.

I headed straight for Beth's door. I only had to knock one time.

"Entre-vous."

I was ready to be one of Celexa's girls.

Chapter 11

Beth made me a runner. She would give me a, "package,"
and I would take it to the street dealer in exchange for money, just
as I had done my first time. Most quantities would be like before.
Three or four ounces for five to seven thousand dollars. The street
dealer would then take that and sell it for a higher price, but that
wasn't my concern. As long as I put the money in my sneaker, I
wasn't worried about being mugged. And the drugs were *always*
disguised.

My first official time running as one of Celexa's girls, I
carried a few economy-sized boxes of Trojans. The box felt
heavier than a box of condoms. If I hadn't known better, I would
have thought Beth was contributing to an underground New
Orleans porn industry. On second thought, they wouldn't have
used condoms so maybe Planned Parenthood instead.

I had been running a few days while still working
downtown and had made sixteen hundred dollars in this time. As
she said, Beth gave me two to three hundred for a drop. She
mentioned that since New Orleans was a, "port" city, and the drugs
were cheaper to access, she could afford to pay me from what she
was making on the mass quantities. I did not ask her where she got
the drugs. Ignorance was the best policy in this case.

The money felt exhilarating and addictive. It was so easy. I was comfortable with my decision. I justified my turn to the dark side as a way to make sure I could pay for my education. I wasn't worried about being caught in New Orleans. Although, the NOPD was known for their own corruption, so I could be in deep shit if I was caught.

Jim called me a few days after my revealing cab ride with George. I didn't return his phone call. School had started back up, and I knew I needed to tell Jackson why I had suddenly left our room, but I really didn't feel like seeing her yet.

I knew the moment would inevitably come when I made plans with a mutual friend, Ashley, who lived in our dorm suite. Well, Jackson really made them for us because she was having one of her parties at her parent's club. Welcome back from Christmas break was the theme. All the apple martinis and cosmos we could drink to remind us of the green and red of Christmas.

Maybe I would meet a new guy tonight at the party and forget all about Jim. But, I didn't want a new guy. I wanted Jim. Only Jim. The guys at the party would be snobby boys from school who thought they were so cool for blowing lines. *Wait a minute. Lines. Coke.* These rich kids spent a lot on drugs. I knew first hand from Jackson.

I threw my designer jeans on that I bought with Darla and Beth. I had already worn them ten times. They were definitely paying for themselves. I could even buy another pair now.

I knocked on Beth's door, and she opened it right away. "You got a run today?"

"Look at you missy. As a matter of fact, voila." She handed me the next drop.

"Beth, how pure is what you've given me?"

"It's mixed some." *Hmm.* I wondered where Beth got her drugs. *I know, I know. I said a page ago that ignorance was the best policy. But I wondered.* Maybe her skeezy boyfriend. If they weren't completely pure, she wasn't at the top.

"You know Calina, if you street deal there are better profit margins." She was such a businesswoman.

"No thanks. Can I borrow your car?"

"Never for a run."

"I just need to go to the drugstore, and I don't feel like waiting for the streetcar."

"Drive safely." She handed me her keys.

"Thanks sweetie." Oh no. I was beginning to sound like her.

I drove to Rite Aid and scoured the shelves for B12 powder. Mixing was the vivid memory I had from Wacky Cracky Jacky. Pinching was the term I used to hear her use. But I had also learned how to make crack from cocaine from a chemistry class, and a Master P song, so I couldn't blame poor Wacky Cracky Jacky for everything.

I wasn't going to inform Beth that I would skim off the top, but I didn't think she'd care. No one ever noticed a little missing. I fended for myself all my life, and college was my ticket to a good job one day, not a store clerk or waitress. I never wanted to end up working back at The Waffle House with my friend Jolene in Ponchatoula. If I was making runs for Beth, I might as well accommodate myself and start an emergency stash. It wasn't like I was going to make a career of it. Jackson's parents weren't the only entrepreneurs on this side of the Mississippi.

I took the powder home. From the three to five ounces Beth had handed over, I would pinch a half an ounce or fourteen grams. In its place, I mixed B12 powder. Then, I took my fourteen grams and made gram packets. At a mark-up of seventy dollars a gram, I could make another nine hundred and eighty bucks in a night of being at a party with other *rich* college students.

I was careful not to pinch more than half an ounce, because I would not want Lidell or other street dealers to have complaints from customers that the product was less effective. I wrapped the drugs in condoms and put them back into the wrapper with a small piece of tape to seal the deal. Touting around safe sex was clever on Beth's part.

I borrowed a Gucci bag from Beth and put on my black cocktail dress. Not so small town anymore. I fixed up really well. I arrived downtown at eleven p.m. Before I could look for Ashley,

Jackson stood arguing with the bouncer threatening his measly minimum wage job. I hoped they made some kind of tips.

Jackson spotted me. "Calina! I'll pay for her entrance." Her parents reduced the cover charge *slightly* when she had a party.

"You don't have to pay for me, Jackson." That had a nice ring.

"It's my party. I'm paying. Get in here. You have some explaining." She grabbed my arm, and I had no choice but to follow or risk a bigger red mark on my arm. She pulled me towards Ashley who sat at the bar drinking an apple martini with our friend Pedro.

Pedro was a rich kid from Colombia. Tulane has a big South American student body. In 2002, its Latin American Studies program would rank second in the country by the Gourman Report of Undergraduate and Professional Programs.

"Cal, what the hell happened to you? Why is all your stuff gone? Where have you been? Are you mad at me for some reason?" It was all about Jackson. She continued. "They changed the locks, and the dorm geek keeps calling me you, and asking where Patty Hearst went. Claims the chick owes a 300-dollar dorm fine." I remembered how I didn't correct Dorm Nerd from thinking I was Jackson. *Woops*. I guessed her parent's people would get that bill soon. I would pay her the money.

I focused on the inanimate granite bar rather than the live soul spewing questions at me. "I had to move out. I'm taking a semester off."

"What? Why? Where are you living?"

"Organic Chem. Lost scholarship. Living with that girl that dyes her hair every week." I didn't want to speak full sentences for the fear that Jackson would interrupt me. I knew living with someone else would make her jealous. She acted upset whenever I made a new friend on campus.

I also wasn't in the mood to rehash the last few weeks for a girl who had just spent two weeks in Hawaii while I slept in the closet and worried about finding a new bed and paying for school. I didn't feel I owed her too much of an explanation since she had been spending less time with me because I, "studied too much."

"You're living with the stripper?" Wow, how did she know that? Guess I was the clueless one. "You could still live with me. You didn't have to move out so hastily." She was probably worried what people would think about her roommate abandoning her.

"Pretend I died. At least now you'll get a 4.0."

"That's messed up. You need therapy. The library called and said you haven't showed up for work." *Woops.* I forgot to tell them I quit. "Where are you getting money from?"

"I got a new job that pays me more. I'll be able to come back next semester. I'm applying for more financial aid, and I'm trying to save in case they cap the amount I can have."

"I don't understand that mess. All I know is you shouldn't drop out."

"You can't stay in school without paying, Jackson."

"You could have worked here at my parents' club."

"I'm not a charity case. It's under control. I'm working at Black Sevens."

"What am I going to do with your bed?"

"Rent it out to the freshman boys who want to be alone with a girl."

"That's messed up."

"That's good entrepreneurial spirit." Pedro interjected.

Jackson ordered two apple martinis. "To Calina's return to school next semester."

Maybe Jackson's parents had gotten through to her that education, not just social standing, was important.

After two apple martinis and catching up with Ashley, it was time to start my selling. I didn't want to be overt about it. Usually it was done in the bathroom. First, I had to find a user.

Bobby Pekarsky. Now that guy was a known coke fiend from Manhattan. His Dad was some big real estate developer.

Last year, when Bobby was the mastermind behind a cheating scandal, his Daddy promised a new ten-million-dollar business school wing. See, money *could* buy security.

Bobby P., as he was called, knew I was a small town girl and didn't give me the time of day, but I thought I would be able to work it with my recent transformation.

"Ashley, let's go talk to Bobby."

"I thought you thought, he, was, like, a slime ball."

"I do. But slime balls can come in handy."

"Do you want to get laid?"

"I wouldn't touch him for all the money in the world."

"Just making sure. Neither would I, so you know he's got to be pretty undesirable."

We made our way over to him, my goods in my loaner Gucci bag. I planned to buy one of my own tomorrow.

Ashley began the conversation. Some boring small talk about vacations. Then, Bobby began to talk about the coke parties in some place called Ibiza. I moved closer to him to whisper. "Do you need any?"

"Huh?"

What an idiot. "Do you want to buy some?"

"From you?"

"Bathroom or not?" I was getting impatient with this kid. He had definitely killed one too many brain cells.

He grabbed my hand and led me to the back of the club where the bathrooms were located. They were unisex with translucent windows where you could see outlines. I moved to the side.

"It's divided into grams."

"I want four."

This was easier than I thought! I decided to increase my price. "Give me three hundred."

"I pay two fifty from my guy."

"Do these jugs protruding from my chest make you think I'm your guy?"

He handed me the money, and I handed over the condom packets. He did some lines on the sink countertop, as I put my money away. He bent over like a horse eating hay, and I wanted to pull his non-existent tail. "My price doesn't include watching you."

He rose and kissed me on the lips, the drugs flowing to his brain fast. "Thanks for making my night more fun." He said as he left the bathroom.

"No prob." I said as I locked the door and squatted to pee.

A minute later, I went back to the party. I was Belle De Nuit, as Beth would say. Her French classes were making her the connoisseur of all things Francais.

Bobby must have told other people about me, because I sold everything the rest of the night and quite a few people got my cell phone number.

Unlike Lidell from Slidell, I made the code phrase, "I have to study for a test." Then the where and what time would follow. I suspected I would be invited to a lot more private parties now. Being popular felt nice, even if it was for a purpose.

After a few more apple martinis, Jackson found me in the growing crowd. "So this is how you're making money? Are you crazy or just stupid? Or both?"

"Remember, I'm working at Black Sevens, Jackson."

"You're a drug dealer."

"No, I'm not."

"Really? Well, maybe you're in denial cause that's not what I'm hearing."

"You've enjoyed sniffing it."

"I sniff and get it out of my possession. You're like, in danger to sell it. It's just stupid."

"So putting it in your body isn't?"

"Well, now you're helping make it easier for me, aren't you?" Jackson stormed off as some guy asked me to dance. She had a point. I wasn't proud of myself for what I was doing.

A guy asked me to dance. Belle de Nuit only wanted Jim. The apple martinis gave me a buzz and made me think of him. He had left more than one message and told me he was getting worried. Maybe I misunderstood George the cab driver somehow. I excused myself from my suitor.

"Can you come pick me up from Forever Club?" He didn't get a hello. I was still pissed.

***

I was quiet during our ten-minute drive. I waited until we were inside his apartment to release my anger. "What's going on between us? I need to know."

"What are you talking about? I thought we were together."

"Are we? I called that cab driver for a ride. The one whose number you left. He seems to know you *really* well. Told me to tell you to bring him girls. So, I'm thinking to myself, who is Jim and who else is he fucking around with? Cause I don't need that shit, you know. I don't want any STDS. I'm a one-guy girl. I have enough in my life to stress about already." *Please G-d, don't let him be a pimp. I promise, I'll...I'll start praying to you for non-selfish reasons.*

"I think there's been a huge misunderstanding. You're the *only* one I'm seeing. That guy thinks I'm a matchmaker cause I'm in the Coast Guard. He thinks we meet tons of women. I swear to you, I'm only interested in *you.* You're pretty hot if you haven't noticed yourself, and I know you're brilliant. You'll get the school thing straight and be very successful. I know it. Come here."

He pulled me towards him. I never believed anyone's promises, but looking into his blue eyes, I wanted so badly to believe.

"George stereotypes us. Eli introduced him to a woman once. He thinks because we're in the Coast Guard that we travel all over the world meeting exotic women. I swear I'm only interested in you. Trust me, I wouldn't even have time to juggle more."

"I'm *that* high maintenance?"

"Aren't all brilliant women?" He winked.

We immediately threw our belongings on the floor and tore each other's clothes off to have make-up sex, or I missed you sex, as if we hadn't seen each other for weeks instead of days.

After we finished, we got up to move to the bedroom. We must have kicked the Gucci purse while on the floor, and a wad of cash fell out.

"What's this?" He asked, putting it safely back in my purse.

"Work money I've needed to deposit." Although it wasn't a complete lie, the words came out of my mouth so quickly I felt guilty because now I was the one who had something to hide.

Chapter 12

From Bobby P., my business took off. My pinching business to my former college classmates was running smoothly. They would rather come to me any day over sketchy sources.

A few weeks later, I was out with Ashley and Jackson at Tom Collins Uptown Bar. Ashley noted, "that guy over there is staring at you."

I spotted Jim looking around the bar and quickly grabbed Jackson. "He never shows up. I need a favor." I slid a canister of tennis balls out of my purse, and told Jackson to open her oversized Prada. "Oh no."

"Come on, if he sees this on me…."

"Damnit, Calina."

Jackson took the drugs. "I don't want to be a socialite in trouble. You know how my Mom acts when I make *Teen People*. If I get nominated for a second consecutive year, both my parents are gonna kill me."

"Yeah, and you can deal with no Sax Fifth Avenue card. Come on, I'm sure there's a new crop of uneducated socialites who'll make the gossip column before you."

"I meant that other guy." Ashley said.

"What?" Jackson and I said in unison.

Ashley pointed to a man with spikey hair wearing oversized cargo pants. Before we could analyze if he was just another bar goer ready to hit on one of us, Jim found me.

"What're you doing here?" I asked.

"You never invite me out with your college friends. Thought I'd drop by."

"We were just leaving. This bar is lame." I had to get him out of there quickly. I couldn't risk any college students asking for drugs.

***

Days later, Mardi Gras arrived. Festivities normally start a month before the actual day arrives. All over the state people attend themed parades with large floats carrying costumed citizens adorned with cheap, plastic, colored beads. They throw the beads along with coins called doubloons and other trinkets to the waving masses. People even fight over the party favors tossed out on a first come, first grabbed basis.

Last year, someone fought me for underwear that said Happy Mardi Gras with two yellow masked faces smiling. Come to think of it, the person kind of looked like Beth with purple hair, so it could have been her since she experimented with different identities. I guessed that came with being a stripper. I would have to check her room for a purple wig.

Last year, I also went down to Bourbon Street and swore I would never go down there again during the Mardi Gras holiday. I was with a male friend that kept stopping to look at women flashing their breasts for beads. I'm not sure why women thought they had to flash for them because I always got plenty thrown at me and didn't strip. I guess it was one of those Mardi Gras myths, although they did have bigger beads and ones with masked faces, so maybe there was some truth to pulling a Celexa.

If you don't keep walking down Bourbon Street, the crowd eats you alive. I ended up getting pushed down on the ground. Not enough showers could rid me of the dirty smell from falling in the street gutter infested with vomit, stale alcohol, and I don't even want to think about what else.

The weekend before Mardi Gras day you can't think about driving anywhere. The parades run at different times throughout the day and night. You run the risk of getting stuck. Most locals leave and take a vacation elsewhere. The partiers left are college students and an abundance of tourists.

Most people opt not to go home at night, but continue to party into the early morning hours. Cabs are hard to come by, and the drivers illegally raise rates. The streetcar runs at odd times and is slow and crowded.

All the madness ends when the clock strikes twelve a.m. on Fat Tuesday, signaling the end of Mardi Gras Day. It's the city's only rest period. *Ever.* Everything from the bars to the stores shut down. Instead of Ash Wednesday signaling the start of Lent and the giving up of something, it becomes the first day of repentance for the debauchery most everyone partakes in the week before. Luckily, the hospitals had to stay open to cover the overdose cases.

This Mardi Gras day, as I expected, Bourbon Street was mayhem. Jim asked to accompany me, but I had to do a run first and made an excuse.

I was almost at block three of seven that housed the clubs, restaurants, souvenir shops, and daiquiri stalls. Video cameras were everywhere recording the jambalaya of sex, booze, and vomit. I'd rather have been sitting in front of a bowl of rice, shrimp and sausage. I covered my head and tried to avoid all the beads flying down from the balconies like lightening bolts from the sky.

I felt a tug on my book bag and someone's hand's around my waist. "I got a girl gone wild." I jabbed my elbow into a person behind me and did a back kick into his shin. The unseen stranger behind me let go, and I was happy I used my kickboxing skills for the first time. "This isn't a semi porn video." I hollered.

Beth and Darla had ordered the *Girls Gone Wild* New Orleans editions of the video series to see if they knew anyone in them, so I knew all about the videos where girls participated in acts deemed immoral by prudes and hot by liberals.

I entered the club. The normal amount of bodies was multiplied by 100 for Mardi Gras. I screamed into one of the security cameras. "I'm coming up!"

I fought my way through the crowd and finally made it to the manager's office to sign in. I wasn't happy about working in the crowd, but I had made so much money during the Mardi Gras season, cocktailing and drug running. A little more wouldn't hurt.

Will greeted me upstairs. "Ready to brave the crowd?"

"No, but I'll deal for the money."

He handed me my shot tray and decided to follow me. "I have to go down and do something about this crowd. This is worse than I've ever seen it."

"Must be a record Mardi Gras." I added.

Will opened the door for me and we entered the mob scene. I began my usual call for shots, adding that they were, "special shots prepared especially for Mardi Gras." None of these tourists would know the difference, and my regulars would understand my need for dialogue variety.

Walking through the crowd was a drag, and I noticed Will carrying a yellow sign with black letters to the front door. "What's going on?" I asked Taco who stood behind the bar making ten drinks at once.

"Looks like we're doing a *real* cover charge now to control capacity. We could bribe the Fire Marshall if we wanna keep packing them in, but it's not worth it, you ask me." He explained.

"So when do you do *fake* cover charges?"

I turned around to greet a new customer. He looked familiar, and I realized he was the guy from a few nights earlier that Ashley pointed out at Tom Collins Uptown Bar.

Here's an interesting one, I thought. His hair was dyed blonde and was short and spikey. His dress was trendy, cargo pants and a t-shirt with Blink 182 written on it. His voice fit his appearance, yet it sounded forced. He looked early thirties trying to be a teenager wearing their pants low. A little too old to be dressing up, acting and talking like one would describe a white rapper before new white rapper Eminem hit the scene.

Eminem made the white rapper phenomenon more popular and mainstream than Vanilla Ice failed to do when he faded into one hit wonder status. This White Wanna-Be Rapper could have come from the still cobblestoned street ghetto, but I didn't buy it.

"I didn't pay nothing to get in. I want to keep it dat way. You seems like you the hizzy for the fo."

"The fo?"

"Info girl. Get wit the program. Name's Leroy." I had known a white LeRoy in Chalmette. His parents just liked the name.

Round Randy approached and his chubby cheeks rested in White Wanna-Be Rapper's face, separating me from speaking to him. "My girl's trying to work. You ain't buying shots, then leave her alone. As you can see, it's busy. Her ass don't have time to chit chat."

"I thought I was talking to her pretty little face, man. I ain't meaning no harm. Just chill."

"Buy a drink or get out. Plenty a other people want to come in." Round Randy made his point and disappeared into the thick crowd.

"Girl, he's wrapped so tight, his ass don't even have a hole. Must be hard on his system. Oh, s'cuse me girl. I shouldn't be talking like dat in front a you."

Little did he know, I had heard far worse growing up. "Look, do you want a drink?"

"Naw. The crowd's my intoxicant girl. But I'll take a club soda."

He was starting to get on my nerves. Without verbally denying him the club soda, I explained, "look dude, I have to go sell shots. It's Mardi Gras and crowded." His way coolness was rubbing off on me. I never called people dude.

"One more question. You got a boyfriend if that ain't your man?"

What an annoying jerk. I waved my hand at him to say never mind you. I didn't care if he decided not to like me and to go buy from another shot girl. I didn't need his money. I had accumulated enough of my own *not* to have to beg everyone to, "please buy a shot."

He must have read my mind. "Seems like you ain't hard up for cash like the other girls pushing the alcohol." I began to walk away as he continued. "I wouldda paid for that soda and tipped you well."

At the end of my shift, I felt hands on my ass, and before I could hit my unseen assailant, Jim whisked me around and kissed me. "Your stubble hurts." His face had gotten a little scruffy the past few weeks. "Maybe work will make you shave if I can't convince you."

"They bent the rules since I just work in the office."

"What are you doing here anyway?" I asked, annoyed that he didn't say he would shave for me.

"Thought I would come down here and surprise my girl."

I was someone's girl. The words made me feel connected to him. I had a moment at that moment. I know it wasn't a marriage proposal or even an invitation to move in, but I felt more connected to him than I had ever felt with anyone.

"You aren't happy to see me?"

I was happy to see him, but sometimes I felt he checked on me too much. Besides, sometimes I didn't want him to ruin my game peddling shots.

We had a drink at the bar, and I turned to find Leroy or as I had named him White Wanna-Be Rapper, staring at us.

"Kiss me really long." I told Jim.

He did and told me, "I missed you too."

I explained, "there's some creep whose been staring at me all night long. Look left thirty degrees."

Jim gave White Wanna-Be Rapper a nasty glare and pulled me onto his lap for a show. We were engaging in major PDA when Will interrupted, "Go keep the jello shots in the walk in cooler company." I smiled and took a seat at the bar next to Jim's.

"What's new Jim?" Will asked.

"No dry spell this month. That's for sure."

"Are you kidding? We never have dry spells." I interjected.

Both men looked at me blankly, as if they didn't know what to say. "You know, some days it will pour for a few moments and then miraculously, the sun will shine."

They both simultaneously nodded, and Jim emphasized to Will that a hurricane would be very good for the city.

"For a city below sea level?" I asked in disbelief.

"You know, growth for the crops by watering the plants."

"More like drowning the plants." *Was my boyfriend drunk?*

"I think she needs another drink, Taco."

"Gotta catch up to your buzz. *Hurricane?*" I mumbled, still in disbelief. *Who the hell would want that?*

We were taking shots at the bar when Kevin and Beth arrived. Kevin went upstairs to the managers' office. After he snapped at me at the Red Room, I never spoke to him again. Jim didn't hang out with him, at least when I was around. Problem solved.

"I forgot my paycheck. I'll be right back and then let's get out of here." The declaration came out before my brain could even think to send the words to my mouth. I wanted to eavesdrop.

Beth took my coveted barstool in the Mardi Gras crowd, and I followed Kevin upstairs.

In the manager's office, I sorted through the checks until I found mine. Two dollars an hour, thirty hours a week was grocery-shopping money that I could use, however, I really wanted to hear what Kevin was up to. I still didn't trust him.

Paul was in the office because I heard him shout, "Fuck Kevin. God damn you. *No* boy. No way. You wanna be one of those stereotypical guys wearing a troop jacket? I've seen that shit on TV."

"Fuck you, Paul. I just know mixing it up more can be cheaper, but it's a hot thing."

"Bullshit, you just want the fucking nod. Just get off the girl and you wouldn't have a problem."

Shit. Was Kevin cheating on Beth with another girl? Or a boy? Was he gay and really into guys? Oh my god, how would I tell her?

It reminded me of George the cab driver asking for girls. Maybe the guys were pimps. Maybe Kevin had guys like Beth had her girls, one pimping sex, and the other pushing drugs. And no wonder I thought Kevin was Paul's nephew. They argued like family.

I tiptoed back to the bar debating whether to mention anything to Beth. I decided to stay out of it. I knew something was awry, I just wasn't sure *what*. When I got back downstairs, Will was busy leaning over the bar, showing Jim something. Beth looked disinterested as she peeled off her fake nails from Celexa's costume, dropping them into a big, plastic Black Seven's cup that Taco had placed in front of her. She was transforming back into nail-bitten Beth.

"What's so interesting?" I asked Jim.

"Will's just showing me the books."

"I didn't know you were into accounting."

"I like business. It's good to understand money."

I understood money all right. It made my world *much* easier. "Let me see those. I can probably understand from the one accounting class I took."

Beth raised her head from her middle finger. "You don't want to see those Cal. It's a lot different in the real world. It might confuse you."

"Thanks for the vote of confidence in what our fine University teaches us."

Will picked up a notebook. "It's the manager's log of how we're running the night. Records of different registers and stuff."

I was already bored when I *should* have been curious with questions, taking care to learn so my brain wouldn't rot while out I was out of school. Lately, I wasn't even reading. I was too tired from the nightlife and just sat in front of the TV during the day. I really didn't want to hear about work after work, anyway. I guessed Will liked to show what he knew and impress my boyfriend with business talk and numbers. Mardi Gras festivities distracted him though, and he had to attend to a fight.

"Let's go. Mardi Gras's a drag." I told Jim.

***

Later that night, I was slipping into my Victoria Secret nightie when Kevin's conversation with Paul reverberated in my mind. I climbed into bed and curled up next to Jim who was reading *The Principles of Accounting*.

"You really *do* want to learn this."

"I always wanted to go to school and my dead beat relative squandered what little my parents left me on business ventures. Shitty thing is, he was successful, just greedy. I never saw any of the money."

"I'm sorry."

"It's okay. I might go back to school after I get out of the Coast Guard. Just have a few loose ends to take care of, and then I might get out."

Speaking of relationships and betrayal, I blurted out that I was worried Kevin was cheating on Beth. Jim put down his book. "What? Why would you think that?"

"I heard him talking about boys with Paul. I think it's another *guy*."

Jim laughed. "You must have misunderstood what they were talking about."

"I hope so, cause that would devastate Beth. I know it would devastate me if I found out you were taking it up the ass."

Jim laughed. "I'd never take it up the ass." He threw his book on the floor and climbed on top of me to get that visual out of his head.

Chapter 13

Mardi Gras came and went like a season. Since New Orleans hardly has noticeable seasons, it was easy to understand how it could magically disappear without a trace. The excitement in the air faded, but the reminder lingered tangibly from the beads strewn all over the streets and hanging from the trees. Intangibly from smells of stale beer and throw up that continued to permeate even after the streets were cleaned. As much as it tried to cleanse itself, the French Quarter never really lost that smell.

A month later, I had made tons of money from running and pinching the drugs. I had over ten thousand dollars in my safe. About fourteen thousand, five hundred to be exact. I had hoarded it in my room, just like I used to do in foster care.

I decided I should put the money in the bank. After all, I was grown up enough to maintain a bank account, and now I had the funds. *Hmm. Funds.* Drop the "ds" and you have *fun.* Exactly what I was having with my newfound money.

I bought Jim a really nice watch. I reassured him that I made plenty of big tips at Black Sevens. He just told me to save up and not to buy him presents. He had gotten even scruffier, and now I thought it was hot and was happy his work had lowered the strict grooming policy. His hair was chin length and he looked a little like a California surfer boy.

One day I rounded up ten thousand to take over to Whitney National Bank. The rest I would keep for emergencies and rainy day shopping trips.

Before I left my place, I got a call on my cell from Pedro. He was an occasional user. Mainly, when he needed a pick me up to study for a test. He had his family's Colombian coffee, but he said this was, "higher octane." He was studying in the B School in cubicle five and I should, "come study too." That was my cue.

When I entered, I found him tutoring Jackson. He told me, "We really need to study for this mid-term." A man wearing a uniform fiddled with the air conditioning unit.

"It's hot as hell in here." Jackson complained as she fanned herself with her hand.

"This room bigger than the five by nine in Orleans Parish."

"I don't care what that is." Jackson whined. "Just fix our air condition unit or you'll go back there."

I looked at the man's scared eyes and said, "that's a jail cell Jackson."

"Oh. Well, in that case, you might end up there with him."

I glared at her.

"I wouldn't mind being locked up with a purdy woman." Uniform Man came to my defense.

"Can you, like, let us study?" Pedro asked Uniform Man.

"Be cool. Be cool." The Uniform Man said and left.

"I'm not sure if he was referring to the air condition or your attitudes."

"I'm sorry, Calina. I'm just stressed over this Finance test. My parents want me to run the family coffee business after I graduate. It's rough for the coffee industry right now in Colombia. I've got to learn as much as I can to help."

I made my exchange with Pedro, handing over a can of shaving cream.

"I'm stressed over Calina's new profession. When are you going to stop this?"

"When I know I have enough to pay for school and be comfortable. The sky's the limit."

"You're going to get yourself into trouble one day. My parents can help if I ask them. It's not a big deal. Tuition's like a water bill on the Long Island estate."

"Well, it's hard earned to me."

"I could say ten grand is for me if you don't want my parents to know it's for you. You know, you've put yourself into the sketchy kid category on campus. You're called classified girl because apparently in that section of the newspaper, there is a place where it says you can get five lines for ten dollars."

"I'm not here to earn a reputation. I'm here to earn a degree."

"Reputation plays a part in the real world. You have morals. How do you feel that it might have been *your* coke that made Sara Randall overdose the other night?"

"Is she okay?"

"If you consider one huge ambulance bill and two freaked out parents okay. If you don't stop, someone's going to get *really* hurt."

Pedro chimed in. "Oh come on. That girl never knows when to stop."

I changed the subject. "Met any good guys lately?" I hadn't been out with her since before Mardi Gras.

"No. Other than just random hook-ups, it's really hard. All the southern ones aren't my style, no offense. I mean, just the other day, I met this one who told me he artificially inseminates cows."

"I hope not with his own sperm."

"Eww, Calina. And all the northern guys at this school, well, they just want the prestige of telling their businessmen fathers that they are dating a Milton daughter."

"As long as it's you and not your ten-year-old sister." I made Jackson crack a smile.

I said bye to Jackson and Pedro and walked to Whitney Bank on campus. I waited in the teller line and filled my deposit slip out by using the hard surface of the wall as my desk. The money sat in my Kipling backpack. Jim bought it for me, and it had a cute little monkey attached to it. Little did he know it was used for drug deliveries.

"Next please."

"Hi, I'd like to open a savings account." The word, "saving," had such a nice ring. I handed the lady with the name tag Teresa the new account forms and shifted my backpack to my front. I unzipped and removed one wad of ten hundred dollar bills. I had already separated each thousand.

"Oh, you have cash."

"Last time I came to the bank, that was an option." I smiled so she wouldn't think I was being a total smart ass.

"How much cash do you have total, sweetheart?" She whispered.

"Ten thousand." I whispered back, wondering why I was whispering too, although I didn't need everyone in the bank to turn and stare at me when I whipped out the volume of bills.

"You might want to think of opening a money market account instead of putting this into a regular savings account. A money market account will accrue interest."

What was she trying to do? Did she think I was stupid? I was in business school before I had to drop out of school.

"Actually, the rates are very similar. I checked."

"Just step over to the customer service desk, and they'll help you from here."

I stepped out of line and over to a desk. A name plate read Marianne Malone. Teresa walked over and whispered in her ear. *Hey, that wasn't very nice. Did I look funny to them? What could they be gossiping about?* Marianne took her seat and motioned for me to come over and sit.

"I'll need you to fill out these papers, as well." She pushed papers in front of me.

"What's a currency transaction report?" I wasn't getting a good feeling from this.

"Just a formality when you deposit more than ten thousand in cash. Did your parents give the money to you to deposit for school?" *Why was this her business?*

"I was raised in foster care."

Marianne walked away and came back with another paper. "Sign here please."

I anxiously read the paper, titled a "suspicious activity report." While I contemplated what this report meant, another bank representative from the back came out front and peered at me. His nametag read, "Danny Toscano." Will's last name was Toscano, too. In the Italian community, Toscano was probably analogous to small town Smith.

I contemplated asking if he was related, but I just wanted to get the hell out of the bank. I realized I had drawn attention to myself by depositing a large sum of cash. No wonder they were whispering and staring.

"Is there a way to bypass this? It seems unnecessary." I asked and told Marianne.

"Why no, and deliberately pulling cash away to avoid filing out an SAR is considered a structured transaction, known as smurfing. Only drug dealers do that."

I was sweating under my tank top. I laughed at her statement. Condescending bitch. I knew more about the street than she would ever know. Unfortunately, I didn't know too much about the bank institution when it collided with the street.

"Of course, you're not a drug dealer?"

I laughed again. "Of course not." I quickly spewed a lie. "Years of babysitting money saved up. I guess now I'll, like, have to pay taxes or something." I was stumbling on my words. I didn't know what else to say. *Did she buy it?*

"Just sign here on the dotted line."

I'm not sure why they always said "dotted" line. There were no dots in this case, only a clear straight line and a clear straight screw up by me.

I wanted to go back to the bank immediately and retrieve my money. It was better off in my own safe where the institution couldn't touch it. I never trusted any organized institutions. I wasn't sure why I chose now to start. I prayed I hadn't ruined everything.

Chapter 14

I immediately went to the library to use the Internet. According to the IRS website, a bank can file a suspicious activity report on, "transactions involving at least five thousand dollars that the financial institution has reason to suspect was derived from illegal activities." Why didn't they teach this kind of useful information in business school?

I waited a few days and then I got something in the mail labeled Whitney National Bank. I stood in the entrance of the house.

"What ya looking at?" Beth asked.

"A hold on my account?" I was about to freak out, but didn't want to in front of Beth.

"Sometimes they do that when you deposit a large amount, but it can also be done on new accounts with as little as one thousand dollars. You didn't deposit a lot did you?"

"Nope. Just two grand." I lied. I was glad this might just be something routine that banks did, although for the next week, I waited for something to happen. After a week passed and the hold was over, I thought I was in the clear.

Another week passed before anything *did* happen. I had withdrawn four thousand dollars over these two weeks and put it back in my safe. I wanted to salvage what I could just in case someone came to take my money away.

I continued to follow my normal routine. Work, Jim, other work no one knew about except for Beth, Jackson, certain druggie kids at school, a few thugs, and Darla. That wack job was also running drugs, however, she was still pinching her own product for herself. That's a big no no in the drug world. *You use, you lose.*

I went to work as usual on a Saturday night three weeks after my bank deposit. Maybe I had overreacted. Maybe everything would turn out fine.

Jim had a cold and told me to give George the cab driver a call, and he would come get me free of charge on account of being tight with Jim. We rode with him when we went out drinking, and Jim didn't want to drive. They spoke Spanish, and that's when I learned Jim was fluent. We never paid George and when I questioned Jim, he would just tell me they were old buddies.

I wasn't comfortable with George since that first ride when he asked about girls, so riding alone with him was the last option I would consider in a bind. I would simply do what Beth had taught me the first night she brought me down to Bourbon Street and walk over to the Royal Senesta's basement and press the cab call button. I was tight with Kurt the doorman by this time.

I left the club at 4 a.m., two hundred dollars richer. I had stuck around for two hours drinking at the bar. Courtesy of my two free drink cards Will had given me, Taco made me two very strong drinks. He knew I wouldn't want to shell out any money beyond his tip. He kept trying to give that back to me.

As I began to walk down Bourbon Street, I heard a voice that I recognized. I turned around to see annoying White Wanna-Be Rapper from Mardi Gras. I began to walk faster. Although he had harassed me that night, I didn't think he'd remember me.

"Hey, girl from Black Sevens."

Think again. I picked up my pace. A bum stopped me. "Can you spare a dollar for an old soul?" I shook my head no. On a normal day, I would have given him five since I was in the black.

"Hey girl, just hang out with me for a little." White Wanna-Be Rapper was still following me.

I kept going. I didn't feel like dealing with this creep. Where was Jim when I needed him? A man tried to stop me. "Sexy thing." *As opposed to human being?*

Two seconds later, a transvestite vampire looking...*now that was the definition of a thing*, told me to, "join the dark side." *Good lord.* I thought I had already joined the dark side. I knew freaks loved to talk to me, but why at the exact time I was trying to get away from someone, did everyone decide they just had to tell me something? Couldn't they give me a night off?

"Girl, I just wanna talk." God, he was relentless.

I entered the nearly empty Royal Senesta hotel. I nodded at Kurt. Just in case, I decided to enlist his help. "Someone's following me. Can you keep him away?"

"Sure. Go on girl."

I headed downstairs as the receptionist hastily explained to a bum that they could *not* sneak them into an empty room for the night. I thought I had finally lost my pest. Surely, White Wanna-Be Rapper wouldn't know to come down to this lobby that served as a secret spot for late night service industry workers.

I was breathing heavily from walking so fast with a buzz. I needed to get in shape. If White Wanna-Be Rapper *did* find me, I wouldn't have help because I was completely alone. I faced the drive where the cabs drove. It could sometimes take ten minutes or more.

A voice behind me said, "well, now we're finally alone to meet the proper way."

I turned around to face White Wanna-Be Rapper. His voice had made a 180 from ghetto to some kind of northern neutral. How had Kurt not been able to keep him away?

"Look Vanilla, I'm tired from being on my feet all night. Perhaps you could buy an actual alcoholic beverage from me one night, and then we'll talk about where you take voice lessons."

"A witty one."

"Just honest."

"That's not the word I would use to describe you."

"I don't even want to know what you would. Nor do I care."

"Well, you should start to. You're in a lot of trouble. So, t-r-o-u-b-l-e, my cherie, is the word I would use for you."

"Glad to know you used hooked on phonics to learn your spelling. I wish all White Wanna-Be Rapper's would."

"When the cab arrives, I suggest you get in, and don't speak. Everyone in this town seems to know someone."

"I'm not going anywhere with you, psycho. I was taught never to talk to strangers."

"Not by your mom and dad Calina Lefevre. Since, you never really had one."

"Excuse me?"

"Eight foster homes, scholarship to Tulane University, roommate was Jackson Milton, now Beth Bloom. You see Calina, I don't drink on the job." White Wanna-Be Rapper flashed a badge and became DEA agent Rick Grant.

"I knew your name wasn't LeRoy."

"That's my brother. I'm Rick Grant. People call me Rick G."

"I don't trust guys with two first names."

"Funny, but this is the real deal. I can give you a number to call to confirm who I am, but I think it will be easier for you if you just cooperate."

He must have flashed his badge at Kurt. Refusing to call him by his real name, I continued to deter him. "I didn't do anything Vanilla. You got the wrong girl."

"Vanilla is too bland. My undercover name is actually Snow-Cone. At least they got some flava."

"You could be called Blanc Mange."

"Don't pull your bayou speak on me. I'm not white cheese. I got it going on."

"Your pick up line when you meet women must be wanna lick my Snow-Cone."

"You know you like them. I've seen your tongue on them down at the Plum Street Snow-Cone stand."

New Orleans was famous for many things, among them, the flavored, frozen ice that encompassed the Snow-Cone.

The cab driver pulled up and Rick G. opened the door for me. I sat on the torn leather seat, wondering whose dirty half covered, or bare ass had rubbed germs there before me. All I could do was picture the bank scene in my mind. *But wait!* Rick G. had been watching me in Tom Collins Uptown Bar *and* in Black Sevens *before* I deposited that money. *What the hell was going on here?*

Ten minutes later, we arrived at an apartment uptown. "Fifteen dollars," the cab driver told us. I folded my arms and stared at Rick G. "I'm not paying for this." I told him, realizing if this was about the bank money, I was pressing my luck. But, I suspected there was more to this late night meeting. If I were only in trouble for depositing money, wouldn't they come to my house or send me some kind of notice that I was under investigation?

"You can't pay with all that money you just made tonight at that upstanding job?"

"Be a gentleman."

"It's only cause you're cute." Rick G. admitted defeat as he pulled out his wallet.

Was he flirting with me? Maybe whatever this was wouldn't be all that bad if this guy could be convinced I wasn't just cute, but a good person and meant no harm.

I took a look around and saw the street sign, "Adams." A few cars with large rims around the deflated tires thumped by playing some rap. "Nice neighborhood, G."

"Not everyone can luck out like you and have a place right on Audubon park."

"More like destiny, not luck." And of course, the fact that Beth had it all planned to make me one of Celexa's girls.

"Just the other day, I had to save a girl mugged at gunpoint in her house."

"The black iron bars on the windows and crowbar marks on the doors make me want to move in."

New Orleans neighborhoods were like that. Make one wrong turn and your ass could be grass. That's lying dead in the grass decomposed for days before someone finds you, and you become part of the earth.

Rick G. opened the door for me and signaled for me to go ahead.

"Look Snowflake, I'm not going inside anywhere with you until you tell me what the hell is going on." I stood still, not budging like my friend's dog that wouldn't walk any further and made you coerce it while pulling on the leash.

"It's more dangerous out here, sweetheart. But as you wish." He pulled out the form I had filled out at the bank.

"Recognize the suspicious activity reports and currency transaction form? That is *your* signature."

"If this is about a bank transaction, why stalk me on Bourbon Street? Seems a bit dramatic." The copy and signature defeated the purpose of me lying. And, the fact that they had cameras in the bank.

"Naturally, there's more to it. If you'll follow me inside."

I conceded. Inside, Rick G. told me I could have a seat on the couch. Nearing five a.m., I was exhausted, but I preferred pacing.

Rick began his explanation. "We've been watching you for a few months now. Since you started working at the club. We've watched a lot of you girls just waiting for the right one to help us. Comings and goings. All movements. Down to your neighbor's Obsessive Compulsive Disorder and the fact that every time she comes home she closes her car door and re-opens it in two sets of four."

"I was wondering what her problem was. It has a name?"

"I can tell you weren't a psych major."

"I'm going back to school. I'll take out some more loans. That's what the money is for. So you see, the government will get it anyway. And, with interest."

"Nice justification. I know you're smart. You've just made some missteps. We were waiting to approach you, but the deposit you placed made it easier for us. Leverage. The bank files a suspicious activity report whenever an employee judges that something is awry. Ten thousand dollars in cash from a young woman looks a little suspicious. FinCen turned it over to us."

"Who the fuck is Fin Sin?"

"Not who, what. Financial Crimes Enforcement Network. They're with the treasury department."

"But you were watching me before this?"

"May I have your attention please? Will the real slim shady club please stand up? Black Sevens is laundering money and drug trafficking."

Shit. "If this is some kind of test of song lyrics, I'm going to be really pissed."

"I'm not in disguise anymore."

"You should pick another one next time. What does Black Sevens have to do with me? I only work there."

But if he had been watching me, then he knew about *more* than my bank deposits. But before I could put two and two together, Rick continued.

"How's Beth Bloom's brothel these days?"

"The sororities did some research. Technically, more than three single girls living in a house is *not* considered a brothel."

"Doesn't matter. In this case, it's not human prostitution or trafficking we're investigating. We've seen you delivering the weird objects. We know the tricks-tennis balls, shaving cream cans -they are all ways to hide drugs in transport."

Uh-oh. I was in deep shit now. "I haven't done any such thing for them."

"Man, you're fit for Hollywood. Don't tell me I'm going to have to take back my statement that you're smart, if you think Beth Bloom is the top of your drug chain."

"She's smarter than you think." I knew Beth wasn't at the very top from the distribution of the drugs and the money involved, but I didn't really care to know who was.

"You can't prove I've done anything." I had become bold in an attempt to cut to the chase and figure out what kind of trouble I was in.

"Look, we could have busted you easily in the act, and we didn't. I don't care if that ten thousand you deposited was drug money or unclaimed tips from your job that you didn't report to the IRS."

Or both, I thought.

"All I care about is you helping us. Work with us, and the bank report is conveniently lost."

"Why'd you pick me? You guys are agents. Can't you send someone in to spy?"

"They trust you. You've been in for awhile. You're a young female. We know you're smart enough and partying with your wealthy friend distracted you from making the grade."

Wow. They did know everything.

"Besides, we don't have any agents that can play your age. We need you to collect information for us. It won't be easy. We need proof."

"Are you going to take my money away or put a freeze on the account?"

"No. That suspicious activity form will disappear forever should you chose to cooperate. But let me make your choice easier. We've taken photos of your runs."

"No jury will believe drugs were in shaving cream cans. That's not proof. And I wasn't doing it for Black Sevens."

"Calina, stop being a naive nineteen-year-old. You were doing it for Beth, but where do you think she began originating her little operation? You, of all people, know nothing in life is free. Beth Bloom didn't pick you by chance. She was looking for girls with sketchy pasts who needed money. I know you realize her tits aren't big enough to bring her the kind of money that lets you get a Visa Black Card."

"So, she has an entrepreneurial spirit. Lots of people do in New Orleans. Big Deal."

"It's a much bigger deal when you're laundering drug money through establishments. Beth Bloom might embezzle through her stockings and lace, but that club you work for is in violation of so many laws. You don't have to be a college grad to figure that out."

"What do you want me to do about it?"

"Work with us, and the SAR is conveniently lost as are the pictures. Look, we're going to get that operation, and if you don't help us, we'll find another way. You'll go down with them as an accomplice to money laundering and drug trafficking. This is organized crime. The big time."

I nodded, having no clue what was in store. Nearing six a.m., the cicadas were making their morning revelry. Through the window, the black night was slowly turning to an orange glaze. My exhaustion was replaced by a feeling of alertness at my new troubles. School was a distant memory.

"If you don't cooperate, I can always show the pics to your boyfriend."

He had me. "At least I have no family members for you to threaten."

"We don't work like that. Those would be tactics of the bar you work for. Have you noticed anything suspicious?"

"Only that on some slow nights when I've asked how much the club made, the numbers were pretty high."

"Well the night you saw me, you noticed something. It was the bogus cover charge you mentioned to Will Toscano. You see, that's one way they can hide dirty money into their accounting practices. We need hard evidence of how the drug money is hidden. I need all the manager's accounting records including register receipts. The ones they *don't* give the bookkeeper."

"Impossible. They keep them locked in a drawer upstairs. The cameras are everywhere."

"You'll think of something clever."

"Why can't you just wear a wire, Snow-Cone?"

"The loud music drowns out line of sight mics. Besides, you're able to go where I'd get caught, like the second floor offices. Keep a camera."

I made another plea. "Can't you leave me out of this?"

"You might not be doctoring bar accounting, but you are inadvertently selling drugs for them. We need hard proof of nefarious activity."

"Tell me what to look for, and who is involved."

"First of all, just keep on with your running for a little while longer so Beth doesn't get suspicious. Just don't pinch to the college kids anymore. I don't want to tell you anything else because the more you know, the more nervous you will be and the less innocent you will appear. You risk blowing your cover when you know too much. Just remember, many are involved. Hold tight, and I will supply you information as needed."

"Like a scavenger hunt."

"Don't people have a pre-set list for those?"

"Not always. Sometimes, one clue leads to another or is given after the first one."

"Well then, like a scavenger hunt."

Chapter 15

Rick G. told me not to tell a single soul what I was doing. No one could be trusted- not my friends, not my boyfriend, not my coworkers. This was organized crime. The big time. I went from small town girl to informant overnight. He would find me when it was necessary. He did give me an emergency pager number if I needed to reach him.

I went home that early morning and slept until two in the afternoon, despite the incessant chirping of birds outside my sunny window and my own tossing and turning with nightmares of what was to come. I saw myself delivering drugs only to turn around and have Jim catch me. In another, I was behind bars. And in the one that woke me up, Jim screamed that I was a criminal.

Someone knocked on my door. "Come in." I mumbled grumpily.

Jim walked into the room with a dozen red roses. "Happy four-month anniversary."

I was a horrible girlfriend. Not only was I hiding my new criminal life from him, I had forgotten our anniversary. He placed the flowers on the desk and leaned over to kiss me. We had decided our anniversary would be the first of every month since he kissed me January first at midnight.

The anniversary was important to me because I had never had any dates of times to remember in my life. Time flies when you're having fun. Or, getting away with breaking the law. I had to let my conscience be free. After all, the system had let me down over and over again. Why should I be faithful to it?

"Get your ass in the shower. We're going to Brennan's." *Mmm.* A good, expensive meal. Just what the conscience police ordered.

***

Sitting in the courtyard over mimosas, my Eggs Benedict and Jim's Oysters Benedict, I decided to find out more about his past.

"How did you live without your family?"

"I don't know." He paused. "My life went on."

His response seemed cold and not like him. I knew he wasn't a heartless person from the attention and affection he gave me.

"I went to live with my uncle. He resented me. Wasn't one for kids. Like I told you, he squandered my college fund my parents left me. I joined the Coast Guard to escape him. I always loved the water and honestly, I identified with our motto, Semper Paratus, 'always ready.' I decided that is how I needed to live my life after what happened. I guess the Coast Guard became my family."

I nodded, thoughtfully listening. "No grandparents?"

"They couldn't believe their only son left could do anything wrong so I stopped talking to them. Mom's parents passed away shortly after the accident."

He raised his glass. "To us. Two kids who grew up without a real family, but managed to turn out ok."

Our glasses clinked. "What do you mean just ok? We're great." *Other than my criminal activity.*

***

Tuesday night, one of my normal nights off, I was called in to work for someone that didn't show. I'd be working with Darla who I almost never worked with because she worked the two nights that I had off. My intuition told me *this* would be an interesting night. Probably, because I was ready to start my new career as an informant.

As soon as I hit the floor, I heard Will talking on the walkie-talkie to Round Randy who sat on his ass upstairs. "Definitely do the cover charge. Just say two-hundred people at ten dollars each. It's a slow night sales wise, and the goods are low anyway."

Well, we weren't low on alcohol. I knew they knew how to run a successful business, cause apparently, according to Rick G., they were running two successful businesses. I followed Will to the front of the club and of course, there was no cover charge initiated at the entrance. Some customers stopped me to buy shots. Will stood talking to a bouncer.

"Look Meyers, it don't always work that way. Some things are out of our hands. But in a few days Paul said he would send something your way."

"Good, cause my girl needs braces. She'll be made fun of if she don't get her teeth fixed like the other kids. Our co-pay on insurance is high."

"I hear ya. If my little girl needed braces, I'd do everything I could to get em for her. It'll be a few days and then, I promise, you'll get your money."

I had heard that Meyers and another bouncer, Donovan, were NOPD. They were grossly underpaid and they made extra money by moonlighting as our security.

The conversations I heard stood out in my mind like voices slowly growing louder, like when I got nauseous from drinking too much and needed to puke.

And Rick G. was correct that I couldn't trust anyone. Apparently, even the cops! who were supposed to be the law enforcers were involved. How on earth was I expected to get proof for him from conversations? That wouldn't hold up in court. *Court! Was he going to expect me to testify?* No way. Then they would know I was the rat and come after me!

Before I could contemplate too hard and look like I was up to something, Darla approached me. "Hey Cal. What's shakin bacon?"

Oh, do I really have to put up with her tonight? Sometimes she could be really fun, but most of the time she was a high maintenance drug addict thrilled to be on display. Maybe I could use her to my advantage tonight. She wasn't the smartest girl I knew. Maybe she could unknowingly help me get the evidence I needed.

"Wanna have some fun tonight?" She asked.

"A night at Black Sevens is always fun." I affirmed sarcastically.

"Here's a pain killer. She whispered. Take it only in good health!" She turned and walked off. What a wack job. It was *just* a pain killer. It wasn't heroin, yet, did it really matter what it was? In life, does it matter what substance you take when you have an addiction? The pill, the blow, the pot, the ecstasy, the alcohol. It's all the same. It's all the *predilection* to the addiction.

I contemplated further. The painkiller might release me from my present worries. But before I could pill pop, Darla was back in my face. "So like, Kev gave me the best drugs ever. I feel so great right now, you can't even imagine."

Kev? Why was she hanging out with Beth's boyfriend? Before I could ask her, Darla fell to the ground, her tray flying in the air. She began convulsing on the ground like a fish on a hook, squirming on a boats slippery deck trying to free itself from its impending butchered death. Her nose began to trickle red.

I quickly looked around. "Will, call an ambulance. I think she overdosed." Will called upstairs on the walkie-talkie and gave Round Randy instructions to, "get help." I stayed on the ground with Darla and tried to calm her body.

"Darla, you're going to be ok." I waited with her until she finished convulsing a minute later.

She mumbled, "Not until the song's over." *Back that Azz Up* by rappers Juvenile and Lil-Wayne played. If you ever went to a club in New Orleans, you couldn't escape the late-90's Dirty South boom.

As usual, the ambulance was southern slow style. Randy came downstairs from his post and told me to move out of the way. He demanded Will come help him on the walkie-talkie.

"I got her front, you get her feet." I followed the two men as they carried Darla out through a side door I had never noticed before and laid her down in a small alley next to a dumpster.

"We don't want her driving customers away." Round Randy told me. *Well, obviously.* I wondered how he expected an ambulance to fit on this narrow street.

"Wait for the car here." Round Randy informed me. *Car?* "When it comes, return to your selling."

"No way. She's my roommate. I'm going to the hospital with her." I looked down at Darla and hoped it wasn't too late for her.

"You want a job, you come back inside."

I looked to Will. He was always the reasonable manager.

"Randy, I think she should go with Darla. You know, she'll tell them she doesn't know what's up. Call us if anything goes sour."

Was Darla's life, a piece of candy? Was she a commodity to them? A possible leak? The managers were definitely in on everything. The men went back inside, and I checked Darla's pulse.

I saw some headlights and looked up thinking it was an ambulance, remembering an ambulance would have emergency music and a blaring light. And, they had sent for a *car.*

A small pickup truck pulled up alongside the dumpster. This could not be our ride. A guy who looked like he came from the docks got out and went to the dumpster and took out a bag that had a Clancy's Fish Co. logo on it.

I heard the clanking of bottles as he lifted a bag out of the dumpster and threw it in the back of his truck. He pulled another bag out that didn't make clanking noises like the bottles, and he dropped that into the dumpster. I hovered over Darla but peered at him as he drove away.

I headed towards the dumpster and peaked inside, discovering another garage bag with the Clancy's Fish Co. logo on it. This bag was full of cocaine wrapped like large stacks of bills.

The headlights of a cab approached as I looked at the time. I moved out of the alley and onto the street as cab driver George got out of the car.

George told me he would put Darla on the ground outside of the emergency room and phone it in. I was to wait and go in fifteen minutes later, saying I was her roommate and heard she was brought to the hospital. My dislike for the operation behind Black Sevens grew.

***

An hour later, I sat in the emergency room, a diet coke in one hand. Two cops approached me. Introducing themselves as officers Jensen and Cooper and speaking very authoritatively to me, Jensen asked, "Are you friends with Miss Darla Roberts?"

"Roommates."

"We just have a few questions for you."

"Fine, shoot." Looking at the guns in their holsters that sat on their waists, I thought, *well don't literally*. I hoped they didn't think I was being sarcastic. I wanted to be cooperative. I was in enough trouble already.

"Were you doing drugs with Miss Roberts?" Cooper asked.

"No." I sounded offended. "We were at work."

"Didn't stop her." Jensen said.

"We work at a courtyard club."

"Don't sass me." Jensen said. "I'll put your ass in a cell." Little did he know, his threat didn't bother me. He'd have to wait in line.

"Do you know who gave her drugs?"

"No." Rick G. had told me not to talk to anyone. I knew police could be involved. I wasn't taking any chances.

Jensen and Cooper walked down the hospital hallway without thanking me for my time, and I decided to follow them to see what *they* knew. I hid behind a corner and heard Jensen say to Cooper, "Found some in her panties. Pure as snow with a speck of dirt. Ninety-percent to be exact. She must not have known how to test it."

Cooper responded, "Or she has a friend in a high place *not* to have had it cut with pharmaceutical powdered milk, Mannitol or simple B-12."

"Maybe they wanted it *that* pure."

Hmm. Darla had said that Kevin had given her the pills, but I bet he gave her the cocaine as well. So Kevin was at the top? I should have known that sleaze ball got Beth involved. But why was Darla with him? Were they simple drug buddies or doing it behind Beth's back?

"I see you're learning how to eavesdrop." I jumped and turned around, almost smacking Rick G. in the face.

"You asshole! I almost wet my pants."

"I would say nasty, but it depends what kind of wet."

"You pervert. Don't sneak up on me like that. And in a public place! You're going to put me in danger. I called Beth about Darla, and she's on her way."

"Just wanted to make sure you've begun to notice that things aren't as they seem at your place of employment."

"What do you think!"

"Come on, let's go in the closet." Rick G. took my hand and led me to a supply closet.

I dropped his hand as soon as I could. "I didn't know five minutes in the closet was your style."

"Well, I outgrew it when I was fifteen. Decided the back seat of the car was more comfortable."

"I don't care to hear about your conquests."

"You started it. I'll make this short before your mentor gets here. We need receipts from the club."

"Receipts?"

"Yes. Copies of when they switch the registers over during the middle of the night."

"Can't you just bust them through poor drug addict Darla and leave me out of this?"

"It's not enough. She'll get out of a possession charge with a slap on the wrist. Seems the kids at your school use some lawyer that contributes to the judge's re-election campaigns."

What a joke. Particularly because Darla only took two classes.

"I'm pretty sure Beth's boyfriend Kevin is at the top of the drug chain."

"You catch on quickly."

"So, if I deliver these receipts to you I'm done, right?"

"When we have all the evidence and then you testify at the trial."

"Oh no. There is no way you're going to make me testify against all these people. They'll come after me. I won't be put in that kind of danger. I saw that *Firm* movie and what Tom Cruise had to go through. Of course, the book was a lot better than the movie. They really shouldn't mess with the novels. I digress. If you're going to put me in this much danger over ten thousand dollars, I'd be safer in jail with the rest of them."

"Look, we'll work something out when the time comes. For now, I need evidence to bust this crime ring. Start out by making copies. But do whatever it takes. I'm going to leave the closet. If no one is around, I'll tap on the door so you can come out."

Rick G. left the closet, and I waited. A second later, he tapped. I waited a few more seconds. I didn't trust this guy. He was going to get me in deeper trouble than I was in already.

I exited the closet as Beth walked by. *Great timing, Snowflake.*

"Hey Cal, what were you doing in there?"

Uhh…..."Re-living my teenage years."

"Alone?"

"Exactly."

Chapter 16

"How's she doing?" Jim asked me the next day.

I squinted up at him in the mid-day sun. He kneeled down next to me, where I laid on a towel, the vast green grass and moss covered trees of Audubon park surrounding me. I sat up and hugged him. "She's fine. Sleeping."

"And you?"

"I'm fine. Just worried." I didn't tell him George picked us up for our hospital excursion. Or how odd I thought it all was. Jim joined me on a giant Polo Bear towel. I flipped onto my stomach to let the sun hit my backside.

"Been hit on yet?"

"No, Mr. Jealousy."

"Doesn't bother me if they look. They just can't have a piece."

I playfully rolled my eyes at him. He knew I liked his cockiness. A squirrel scurried up a tree with something, and I stood up to investigate. I pointed up to the tree. "Look. The squirrel is eating a lollypop."

Jim stood behind me. "That's cute. But these are even cuter."

He took my hands in his. "I think they forgot to grow up."

"You're sillier than that squirrel. He's actually pretty smart. He probably went into Rite Aid when someone held the door open New Orleans slow style and then picked out the flavor he wanted."

"My intelligence isn't that far behind him. I went into Black Sevens and picked out mine."

"Glad to know I'm a lollipop." I kissed him. The constant attention he gave me and the care he took in knowing everything about me from my hands to my ass to my ankles, to my love of ice cream, made me want him more.

"How do you know that squirrel is not a *her*?"

"Just look. He's licking the pop, not sucking it."

"Come on, perv." I led him to the house.

Once inside, Jim went into the bathroom and hollered to me. "Ah, shit Calina. I told you to throw out this mirror. I just cut myself on the fucking thing."

"I'm sorry. I forgot." I had broken a mirror and still kept it by my sink to check the back of my hair to make sure every inch was straight after blow drying. I got up to find him a Band-Aid, but he had already gone into the cabinet below the sink.

"I didn't know you played tennis."

I looked down at him kneeling on the floor. *Quick thinking, Calina.*

"We have courts on campus."

"When are you going to teach me?" The only thing I knew about tennis was that it involved swinging a racket.

"I need to shower and get ready for work."

"I don't think you should work at Black Sevens anymore."

"Why? I'm not in school right now. I need to make money."

"I can help you with school."

"That's ridiculous. Scoot. I'll call you tomorrow." Jim left my bedroom, and I got into the shower. Rick G.'s, "trust no one," echoed in my mind like those cheesy scenes in soap operas where the character's flashback to a previous conversation only to remind the audience what they missed. I wasn't sure why they did that when the plots were so slow anyway.

How could I know if *I* could even trust Rick G.? After all, he called himself Snow-Cone. I laughed out loud, but it was one of those nervous laughs. One of Jim's most endearing qualities was his attention to detail, but maybe it was his scariest. I trimmed my hair less than a half an inch and he noticed. Maybe he knew that I wasn't such a good girl.

When I left my room to head out for work, I heard arguing in Darla's bedroom. Her door was slightly ajar, and I could see her on the floor one knee on the ground, the other at a ninety-degree angle.

"What the hell are you doing, Darla? I want to talk now." I heard Beth's agitated voice.

I saw Kevin standing next to Beth. His complexion was sallow and he kept itching himself and fidgeting, clearly antsy in his own skin.

Darla answered Beth's inquiry. "I hurt my hip flexor when I fell during my seizure. The upper thigh tightens, and it really hurts. My physical therapist said I'm supposed to do this stretch. I can't sit with my legs crossed for a while either." She sat back on her bed and demonstrated, opening and closing her legs in and out, like she was using an old Suzanne Sommer's Thigh Master.

"Well at least you won't have to quit your day job."

"What're you talking about?"

"I know you two are doing it behind my back."

"I didn't sleep with your boyfriend. We just bond over certain things."

"Drugs, you fucking addicts."

"At least I have no more icky nose hairs."

Kevin looked more alert now. "I wouldn't sleep with a girl who is too stupid to realize she just became another statistic to the narc cops who track what drugs move through this city."

Beth gave it right back. "You're one to talk. You use so many drugs you can't keep your dick up. Maybe if you spent more time getting the goods and managing your street dealers instead of using, *this* wouldn't have happened."

I hoped he didn't know that *I* was on staff as a street dealer.

Beth stormed out of the room, shutting the door behind her. "Calina, I've been worried about you. Kurt told me someone was following you the other night."

Shit. I convinced her the bellman at the Royal Senesta mistook me for someone else. *Damn, Rick G.* I definitely couldn't trust him to keep me safe.

***

When I got to work, bouncers Meyers and Donovan were at the front door. A white guy wearing a sleeveless hoodie was trying to gain admittance. He had a tattoo that read, "peace," on his right shoulder. Meyers told him, "You ain't wearing the proper attire to gain admittance."

The white guy answered back. "Oh yeah? What's that?" He sounded drunk.

"You can't go in with a hoodie, punk." Drunk Guy took a step forward. Meyers told him to take a step back.

"What you gonna do bout it, po po. You *off* duty."

How did he know that? Maybe Meyers had that cop look. Meyers responded, "Don't test me, punk."

Drunk Guy responded back, "This isn't *your* club."

"It sure as shit ain't yours."

"I know who you work for. Wouldn't want to get in trouble with the boss, would ya?"

"We are cops, dumb fuck. *We* are the *law* in this city."

"Is everyone in this town is a shit kickin' hick?"

"You're gonna find out what getting the shit kicked outta you feels like."

"Fuck you, pig."

Drunk Guy went to punch Meyers, and Meyers took him down. Donovan joined in, and Drunk Guy ended up pinned to the ground.

"You wanna go to jail, punk?"

This was way too heated for a club admittance, and I ran to find Will who thought I looked, "spooked."

"Fight. Outside." I said quickly. Will took off after me. When we got back, Meyers had a knee in Drunk Guy's back. He laid face down on the ground. Donovan was on top of him too and held his feet down. One of his friends shouted, "Let him go."

A bystander screamed, "He can't breathe."

Will screamed to break it up. "Meyers, Donovan, lay off!"

Another friend found an officer on horseback. "We need help. Over here." The Officer walkie talkied, "Call the 8th district."

Will pulled the bouncers off and told Drunk Guy to get up. There was no movement and after a minute, Will rolled him over and poked him. He was pale and still. Will shouted on his own walkie talkie, "Call an ambulance." I had now heard that twice in one week.

Realizing I could not do anything else to help, I went to sign in for my shift. I noticed it was close to the time I discovered the drop that occurred the night Darla overdosed. I asked Taco to bum a cigarette to have an excuse to go out back. I occasionally did this, but had recently declared I quit. Everyone was always saying that and going back to the cancer stick, so I didn't think my actions were suspicious.

I went out the side alley door. I walked to the next club's dumpster and hid behind it. I had bought a miniature, disposable, pocket camera from Rite-Aid and took it out where I had it hidden in my bar apron. *Tick tock. Tick tock.* Where were these guys? Luckily, no manager would be checking on me right now due to the situation at the front of the club.

A minute later, I heard the truck. I peered around the corner. I began to snap some photos. When the truck drove away, I got up, looked around, went to the dumpster, and snapped some more photos of the big cocaine drop from Clancy's Fish Co. or at least, that's where the logo said it was from.

A few minutes later, I thought the coast was clear, when I heard a truck drive up. Kevin got out and took the bag from the dumpster. Figured. No big surprise there. I snapped his photo.

"What the hell was that light?" I heard him ask his driver.

I hid deeper behind the dumpster, my heart racing. I was convinced he was going to kill me if he found me.

"Come on man, let's go." The driver hollered. When I heard the car door shut, I slowly peaked around the corner. As they drove off, I took a picture of the license plate.

When I returned inside, I saw Will standing by my shot tray that I had left at Taco's bar. "It ain't my job to guard your inventory. I have more important situations to deal with." I knew he wasn't suspicious of me when he had the drama at the front of the club to contend with. But someone else was.

***

Taco asked if I wanted a ride home that night. I wouldn't have to pay a cab, and a ride would beat waiting on one. Taco was hungry and wanted to get a bite to eat at a late night diner.

"Ever heard of the King of Cocaine?" He asked me over his eggs.

I stared at him blankly. He continued. "Wealthiest criminal in history. Estimated thirty billion in net worth?"

I continued to stare at him blankly, but offered up, "Master P was one of wealthiest men under forty last year." Now, it was Taco's turn to stare at me blankly. I responded, "He's a local rap artist, so I know him."

Taco nodded and began his tale. "The King of Cocaine was Pablo Escobar."

"Oh him." I didn't want to seem completely clueless, and I had heard his name before. All I knew was something about scary, bad man and drugs. I decided to pay attention.

"I worked for him."

"You what? You're shittin' me."

"You know I'm from Medellin, Columbia. That's where Escobar grew up. He was good to the poor. Gave many of my friends and family money. Many of those friends and family were also killed. I helped launder drugs for years, but I was tired of the violence they brought.

If you objected in any way or wanted out of the business, you were, well how they say, 'dead meat'? Escobar killed anyone and anything that got in his way. In 1989, he even put a hit on a presidential candidate, Luis Carlos Galan Sarmiento.

I had made enough money and decided to move to the United States. That's when I landed in Texas and met Jamie Castillo who escaped Waco when it went down. Played guitar with him and Koresh, but that's another story. The point of my story is that people with money and power get greedy for more.

After the Medellin Cartel went down in 1993, the Cali Cartel rose to power. Now, we're on the Norte del Valle Cartel. You better believe the drugs coming into New Orleans are from *this* cartel and Columbia. Columbia is the second biggest cocaine producer behind Peru. This will never end because it's a cycle that keeps going. Just don't get involved with anything with drugs, Calina. You are too young, and I don't want anything bad to happen to you. If you see something in the club, just pretend you didn't."

I nodded quietly to his advice.

***

Twenty-four hours later, I knocked on the door of the house where Rick Grant had first enlisted or entrapped me. He opened the door before I had a chance to ring the bell. "What you doin up in here, girl?"

"Oh, I see you're undercover playing Snowflake, but your DMX routine is pathetic. And, word on the street is Snowflake takes it up the ass."

"I can always tell when girl's in a snappy mood."

"Maybe you're on drugs when you revert back to White Wanna-Be Rapper. Maybe, you're in on this whole drug thing."

"Not quite, Calina."

"How fast you change back to normal dialogue. Multiple Personality Disorder. I don't have to have a psych degree to know that one from those cheesy lifetime movies or my favorite soaps, of course. Remember *Santa Barbara*? That was the best. I want to go there someday."

"It's really a place called Burbank, and it's dry and ugly. Doesn't have the same character as your old swamp land. Come on in. You don't want to miss the news."

I followed Rick G. inside where he turned the TV on. I took a seat. The local reporter started with the breaking news. "On a street that should be safe for tourists, a man dies. A young college student from Loyola died at Bourbon Street Nightclub, Black Sevens, last night. His parents are asking questions and not only suing the club for wrongful death, but the NOPD as well."

Rick G. commented, "Who did they think he was, the Unabomber?"

"They called an ambulance. I didn't find out what ended up happening. I was too busy trying to exonerate myself."

"He was DOA. What you need to know is they found Beth Bloom's missing roommate."

"Oh?"

Rick G. stared at my blank face as I waited for him to tell me where. "Girl, you don't get it. They found the roommate that went missing."

"I don't have time for your shit."

"The young college student from Loyola, James Foley, is dead."

I shuddered as I put two and two together and realized Rick G. was telling me the tourist killed at the club was in fact Beth's old roommate.

The Mayor came on TV. "In Louisiana, committing a misdemeanor that contributes in any way to death is homicide. It's called felony murder. A citizen may only detain or confine someone who has committed a felony, not the misdemeanor of throwing a punch."

A reporter asked a question, "But Mayor, wouldn't you argue that an off duty officer carries more privilege than your average citizen?"

Rick G. commented, "Bullshit." He abruptly turned the television off. "So, how are the receipts coming?"

"Really? You're going to ask me *that* when you tell me that little tidbit of information that *I* could be next?"

"We have no proof they murdered the kid."

"We will when the autopsy report comes back as *suffocation* not intoxication."

"I love it when you rhyme girl."

I threw the package of photos at him. "I just went to the one-hour photo for you. I expect reimbursement."

"Tell it to the judge."

Rick G. opened the photos and started going through them. "Man girl. Good job. But if you get more photos, bring me the roll, and I'll develop. Never know who works in the drug store."

I thought back to my bank excursion and the man with the nametag Toscano. I shivered. I needed to find out if the guy was related to Will.

"Now I need some written stuff. The kind of information the IRS would love to get, but can't be there to physically count themselves."

Chapter 17

I left Rick G.'s apartment pissed. He was crazy. Insane. Delusional. Out of his mind. There was no way I could just get proof so easily. I could see it now. *Excuse me, Will, can I borrow that register report and make a copy for the U.S. government? They'd really appreciate it. It'll only possibly incriminate you.*

I did think of something that would make it easier for me to get up close and personal to the information. When I was with Jim, I asked. "Babe, can you use your friendship with the guys to get me a beer tub position? Will loves you."

"After what happened the other night, I want you to quit."

"But being behind the beer tub will keep me out of harms way. It's hard to get a beer tub position unless you're sleeping with a manager. I guess they think it's like a Hollywood casting couch."

"That shit happens everywhere. I'll talk to Will. See what I can do. But I really want you to quit that bar soon. It's bad news."

***

Jim came through. *Fast.* The next night at work, Will told me I had been promoted to a beer tub girl. "Your boyfriend worries about you on the floor."

I would now be in charge of a register. I could figure out what to do to collect evidence, and get Rick G. off of my back. I silently cursed him for making me use my boyfriend. Then again, I had no one to blame but myself for the underworld I had entered.

Beer tub girls had a good, laid back gig because everyone came to us for drinks, and we didn't have to walk through the crazy, drunk crowd. I was over that. I had paid my dues as a shot girl.

My first night in this new position, I came to better understand how the drug money was hidden in the club. I began working at four p.m., as opposed to my normal eight p.m., because the beer tub girls had to arrive at work for happy hour.

The register manipulation began when Will came over to do a Z out on my register. I had worked in enough retail stores growing up to know that the Z out was done at the *end* of the night to close out the register, and that he *should* have been doing an X out if he wanted to check sales figures in the middle of a shift.

"You're a great boss, Will."

He tilted his head and looked down at me. "You on X tonight?" He referred to the drug ecstasy or MDMA, Methylenedioxymethamphetamine, that made people touchy feely and have heightened senses of euphoria. Most club partiers would declare their love for one another. Drugged on the job wouldn't have been a stretch in New Orleans.

"No silly. I've just never told you that. Thanks for my promotion."

"My pleasure, girl. You're not a pain in the ass like some a da girls. Never know what tricks most have up their skirts." He winked at me. I felt ill. *Did he somehow know I was spying?* I remained calm and focused on my task. I watched him move his hands adeptly on the register keys.

Before he pushed the register key to do the Z, Will rang in five hundred cover charges at ten dollars each. I looked toward the club entrance and saw *no* cover charge sign. Five thousand pretend dollars in the register? The register printed a close out receipt for Will. I had to get my hands on that receipt. The cover charge was the perfect way to hide drug money. No one could monitor the cover charges a club did or did *not* collect and as a tourist club, the numbers were feasible.

I learned the second way the registers were manipulated, when Will came back to my register. I obliviously pointed out that the register said seven p.m. when it was really eleven p.m. Will offered up the information I sought when he had the opportunity to sound like the expert. "The register *thinks* it's seven p.m. It thinks it just went through another happy hour."

"Oh." I continued to act naive, but my business sense was flying in my head like a bird headed from NY to FL in the dead of winter. If we just had another happy hour, but we really didn't, what did that mean?

During happy hour, from four to seven p.m., customers could purchase three beers for the price of one. That was 3 beers for $5 versus the normal $15. After happy hour, beers would go back up to $5 a piece. If the club wanted to hide money during normal hours, Will could mark the register tapes for the accounting department as 3 for 1 and make it look like nine beers went out for fifteen dollars when it would really be $45. So, $30 in extra money was not reported as income for taxes. The nine beers is a small-scale example.

That night, after happy hour, I sold five hundred beers. That meant twenty-five hundred dollars, but the bookkeeper would think the club only made fifteen-hundred dollars. One thousand dollars was hidden, on record as a false happy hour. The manipulation occurred *every* night in some fashion.

The cover charge scam was a better way to hide the drug money. In addition, the shot money never went into the registers. Simple acts of genius or *corruption,* to hide money. Just by manipulating register tapes. I needed the managers' logbook with copies of the receipts the bookkeeper never saw.

I thought of a plan. Flirting with some idiot wouldn't be *that* hard. I was in luck and the New Orleans Brass Hockey team had just won a game. They were part of the East Coast Hockey League starting in 1997. They were mid-level professional ice hockey players in a tier below the American Hockey League.

When the Hornets moved to New Orleans and wanted them to pay for converting the arena to and from hockey to basketball after each game, the ownership didn't want to take on the expense. They folded in 2002.

These guys thought they were hot shit. "Name's Fred, sexy lady."

"Well Fred, I hope you plan on staying til closing time. Who knows what's in store."

Slut. I hated Rick G. Maybe once I had to enter witness protection, I would go to Hollywood and begin my career as an actress since my current skills would win me an Oscar. Sure would defeat the point of the program, but I wasn't expecting the institution to take care of me.

"You're coming home with me tonight." Fred emphatically and drunkenly informed me. Easy to have plans go your way in a town of sleaze. Luckily, they'd be *my* way instead of his. At my five-minute break, I called Jim on my cell phone to tell him I didn't like the way a customer was acting. He should come and get me.

I whispered to Hockey Player that I would do unspeakable things to him if he just waited until I got off of work. At two, Jim walked into the club. When I stepped from behind the beer tub, Hockey Player grabbed me and wouldn't let me out of his arms. I felt so humiliated I had to get close to this disgusting jerk.

Jim approached fast and tore Hockey Player off of me. I headed upstairs as the two guys fought. On Sunday nights the floor manager would also close upstairs. Will was looking into the cameras and turned around when he heard me. "Jim needs help fast."

"What the hell is goin on?" Will asked rhetorically as he stormed downstairs. "I got bouncers for this."

I sat at his desk. I didn't have long because I saw on the computer monitors that the bouncers were in fact, breaking up the fight. Since Meyers and Donovan were on a, "leave of absence," from the club and the police force, I was hoping these new guys didn't know what they were doing.

I looked up and saw a camera pointed on me. *Shit, this was new.* Paul must have heightened security after the incident, or *murder?*, at the front of the club. I couldn't take evidence now. I stealthily looked around slowly, careful *not* to bring attention to myself if Paul was at home watching the cameras.

Will had left the managers logbook open on the desk. I saw the shot girl productivity sheets we had to sign out for. I needed some of those since the shot money wasn't recorded. I also saw a box on the desk with what looked like register receipts.

I watched the video monitors. I heard Will tell a bouncer to kick Hockey Player out. He then headed back up the stairs. I sat at the desk, touching nothing. "What was that all about?" Will asked.

"I don't know. I think he just wanted a piece of ass and mine was prominent."

"Well, your boyfriend has a black eye. Better get him home to ice it."

***

I hadn't foreseen laying an ice pack on Jim's eye for the remainder of the night. He whined and wanted some ice cream. He was a baby when he didn't feel well, but he deserved all I could give him since it was my fault.

In the morning, he wasn't happy. "Why did you lead that psycho on last night? Are you trying to make me jealous? Do you think I don't put enough into this relationship?"

I thought I was having a dream until I fully woke, and remembered the previous evening.

"What?"

"Will said you were flirting with that sleaze bag last night."

Will sold me out? My subtlety skills weren't as good as I thought. Or maybe playing two roles at once was too difficult for me. My Oscar hopes faded to a daytime Emmy. "I was trying to get a bigger tip. You know how it is."

"I'm a little sick of your obsession with money, Calina. You're fine. Stop trying to extort everyone."

Was this our first fight? I sat up, hurt by his remark. "I'm not obsessed with money. I need it for my future in school."

"I can help you with school. Money isn't *that* important. You seem a little more stressed lately. What gives?" He really did read me *well* because I thought I had been sufficiently hiding the government informant stress until now.

I tried to turn it on him. "Maybe when you *have* money it isn't as important. I'm gonna go home." I got up and threw my clothes on. I wanted to tell him everything before I left, including why I was acting stressed and not like myself, but my throat felt choked and dry from my attempt to keep from crying. I couldn't risk ruining the one perfect thing in my life, despite our present dispute. I didn't think Jim would understand my dislike of the institution that let me down as a child as a justification for dealing drugs.

***

"I have a month long managers' log for you. Shows how they manipulate the books. Seems the club is also hiding some of their own profits to avoid paying taxes." Later that day, I bluffed about what I had to Rick G.

"Hand it over. I can't wait to get these SOBS. This case is going to make me big. I'm gonna write a true crime novel."

"It's hardly the Manson murders. I'm not giving you anything."

"Jail is no place for a young woman. Especially in New Orleans. You thought small town living from home to home was bad. Wait til you're locked in a cell with angry, hormonal women."

"Fuck you. I actually want to be back in school, so that's my first demand. Things were a lot easier, even with Organic Chemistry. I want money for four years at a good school somewhere far away. I'm doing something *very* dangerous. If Will realizes the exact time when the log went missing, he'll know *I* took it. You're lucky to have me. The only reason I knew about the log was because he showed my boyfriend one night."

"Why do you suppose he did *that*?"

"Will likes to impress people with business. Makes him feel smart."

"If you say so."

"What's *that* supposed to mean?"

"Nothing."

"Good. Then I want to see proof of my demands being met."

"And where do you want to go to school? A small town, remind you of your roots before all of this?"

"No. Small towns are where they find you and put a bullet in your head. I want another country. The Sorbonne sounds nice.

I'm fluent from taking French for many years. Figure I'll pick it up fast."

"I'll see what I can do. But without those logs, I don't know if your bluffin' about the information you have."

"Oh, you mean your, "fo," in White Wanna-Be Rapper language? Yeah, well seeing as you're the one who hid out in the club and watched what was going on, you know I'm not bluffing. But you know what? Find me when you're ready to negotiate for real."

I left mumbling about first my boyfriend, now the freaking agent, who else wants to piss me off?

Later that evening as I was online looking at other colleges throughout the country on my laptop I bought with drug money, Jim entered my bedroom without knocking. I quickly pushed the X mark on the Netscape browser. I had not yet contemplated separation from him.

"We're going away. Pack whatever you want. It doesn't matter."

"I thought you were mad at me?"

"Just promise me never to talk to a sleazy guy again, and it's fine. I got you a few days off, and we're going away. We'll be completely alone."

***

We drove for four hours and entered Pensacola Beach, Florida. Jim's uncle had a one-bedroom condo right on the beach! He said using the beach condo was the only thing he borrowed from his uncle, since he rarely spoke to him. You literally could open the door, step on a patio, take one more step, and be in the sand.

The sand was so beautiful, all white and fluffy. I wanted to lie on it without a towel. When my feet touched the water, I screamed like I did when someone in the house got in the shower when I was already in mine and made my shower water turn cold!

That night, Jim made my favorite, pesto pasta, and we dined on the patio. We drank wine. The waves made their hypnotic crash in the background. It couldn't get any better than this. "When am I going to meet your uncle? He can't be *that* bad. He has good taste. He must do well for himself? What kind of business is he in?" I asked before twirling the pasta around my fork and taking a bite.

"That's a lot of questions." He smiled and continued. "Service Industry. He's no one worth meeting. He's selfish."

"But, he's your only family."

Jim moved in his chair, and it skidded against the patio pavement. He rose and went inside. He came back out with a tiny blue box that, by now, I recognized as a Tiffany's box. He knelt beside my chair. I dropped my fork and gulped the pasta I had been slowly chewing.

"I was going to wait until our last night here, but since you brought up family, I know the timing is perfect."

I couldn't say anything. I felt as stoned as I had been after opening the last Tiffany's box Jackson had left me.

"Calina, I want us to start the family we both lost. Will you marry me?"

"I can't believe this is happening. You were so mad at me this morning, and now….."

"The incident last night just pushed me forward. I don't want another guy to touch you ever again. But, it's not because of that. I bought this a few weeks ago."

"So this isn't to make me or you feel secure?"

"Don't be ridiculous. I love you. Before I met you, I was obsessed with work. Now, I have something else to look forward to everyday. I admire you so much. You pulled yourself out of the system. I love you."

"I love you too." I had never had anyone want me around this long, besides Jackson, but I didn't call that love, more like control.

"Um, my knee is starting to hurt."

I gave him a hand and had him rise to his feet. I stood too, looking up at him. "Calina, your hesitation scares me."

"The answer is yes."

The concept was so foreign to me, I had to force the words.

"Yes?"

"Yes. I will marry you."

He slipped the gorgeous, sparkly ring on my finger, and I kissed him. We sat back down as I fawned over my ring, and he explained its details. It was platinum, more expensive than gold! I had never seen something so gorgeous before. I sure did have fun whenever I got a Tiffany's box.

After dinner we chilled on the beach, and Jim insisted we bring a towel. "Why did you hesitate earlier, Cal?"

Why did I hesitate? For some reason, marriage made me uneasy. I hadn't seen good examples growing up, so tying the knot seemed scary. But something deep down was bothering me, and I didn't know what it was. Perhaps I was scared about my troubles and how everything would work out. I would find a way.

"I guess I'm so young, and it was so unexpected."

"We can take things slow. I know you want to finish school and have a career before kids, and that's totally cool."

"Well, before we even get close to tying the knot, we will have to get you a hair cut. You can't even see your face anymore. I really don't understand why they bent the rules for you."

"They changed the policy. Eli has long hair now too."

We began to make out on the beach and took it into the condo to have that wild sex that you claim was the best ever. But it really was! We were both so intense after the proposal. I had given myself to him in ever way possible-emotionally, physically. Except of course, for the truth that I was in trouble.

When we collapsed on the bed, Jim told me, "I really don't want you to work at the club anymore. I'm sick of all those sleazy guys harassing you."

Uh-oh. I had to stay in that club as long as possible or I wouldn't be able to spy for the government.

Jim continued, "I can help you financially. I make enough money."

He couldn't make *that* much in the Coast Guard. "Did your uncle ever give you any of your money back? It doesn't look like he squandered it too bad with this place."

"No. I'm not an inheritance kid or whatever you call them."

"Trust fund babies. Like my friend Jackson."

"Right." He changed the subject back to me. "So you'll quit the club soon?"

"Soon. I'd like to save money a little while longer."

"You can move in with me now and save money."

I held him off for one month with the excuse that Darla and Beth would need time to find another roommate. I needed to get away from their sketchy asses, but I also needed to stall quitting the club.

Jim fell right to sleep, but I couldn't yet. I got up and decided to sit on the patio for a few minutes to listen to the gulf's waves. Whoever owned this place had to have some major loot.

Spring was still with us, and the night air was still chilly. I needed a sweatshirt to put over my nightgown. I didn't want to wake Jim rifling through my still packed suitcase, so I went to the living room to see if his uncle kept any sweaters in the drawer. I pulled each drawer open and finally found a big New Orleans Saints sweatshirt at the bottom. When I lifted it out, I found papers underneath it. I decided to be nosy. I was already undercover, what would this hurt?

The papers didn't make any sense to me. There were a lot of numbers talking about a street tax to cops, and I recognized the names of moonlighting cops working outside of Black Sevens, Meyers and Donovan. Hmm, so they definitely knew drug laundering was going through the club and were paid off. I found another paper with some Coast Guard routes detailing transit zones through South American countries. Columbia was one and it reminded me of my conversation with Taco.

Jim must have left the papers in the Condo from a previous time spent here, but he told me he didn't work on a boat. Maybe he got them in the office since he did paperwork? Maybe he was investigating how the drugs got into the city? I shook off a chill. I decided to forget sitting outside and placed the sweater back in the drawer. I turned the lights off and headed back to the room. I buried the papers under my clothes in my suitcase.

Chapter 18

"I'm not pinching anymore." I told Jackson as I lay on my old bed. I wished I could just escape my new life and return to the way things were, before I lost my scholarship money.

"You finally got some sense in your thick mind?"

"You mean skull?"

"Whatever. I like to flip clichés. What made you wise up?"

"I can't say right now."

"Don't be obnoxious, Calina."

"I'm serious, Jackson. I wish I could tell you more than anything, but it has to wait."

"I can't believe you're going to get married. And he bought you a decent ring for a Coast Guard."

She was careful not to say *big* ring, because she would have wanted one a hundred times larger.

"You did well for yourself. But, I think you're too young to get married."

"I'm going to be twenty soon. It's not like I'm fifteen and pregnant like the girls from home."

"Don't even talk about preggers. I hope you wait until you get out of school."

"I'm not having kids yet, don't worry."

My cell phone rang just as we were about to put *Dumbo* in and smoke weed. As if I needed more paranoia.

I answered the phone. "My little Calina. I haven't heard from you in quite some time. Heard you were spotted in Pensacola Beach. You really shouldn't sit outside in your pretty blue negligee. Not that you don't have a great body, but you just never know who's watching."

My face turned bright red. That son of a bitch. I looked at Jackson. She could tell I was uncomfortable because she whispered, "who is it?" I put up a finger to tell her to hang on for a minute.

"Meet me at Camellia Grill in twenty minutes. None of your illegal crew hangs there. Except maybe Darla for her chocolate cherry shakes, but that's at four in the morning. Now wish Jackson adieu."

He hung up before I could damn him to hell. I felt violated. I turned to Jackson. "I can't watch *Dumbo*. I'm really sorry."

I headed for the door. "Where are you going? Who was that?"

"I'm sorry, Jackson." I was out the door headed for the streetcar. Camellia Grill was about half a mile from school, but by the time I walked to the streetcar and waited for it, it could take me a good thirty minutes.

Rick G. sat at the counter wearing a New York Yankees baseball cap. I sat down, pretending not to know him. If I was going to feel like I was in a movie, I might as well play the part. "I'll have a cheeseburger and fries." I whispered to Rick G., "that's definitely on you. And don't you know, Yankees suck. Red Sox are much cooler."

"If you like a team with a curse on them. I guess I saved you from watching *Dumbo* stoned."

I slammed my fist down, and my fork flew behind the counter, barely missing a chef. I turned to face Rick G. "I'm not helping you anymore. I'd rather go to jail. Why on earth would you bug Jackson's dorm room?"

"Watch that temper. We've got everything bugged. Even the cheapest of the Milton homes. Couldn't they have gotten her a house on Saint Charles rather than that old dorm?"

"They want her in an environment where she can learn and not throw parties every night."

"Then they shouldn't have picked New Orleans and Tulane University as the place to send their kid."

"It *is* the Harvard of the South."

"What's that on your hand? Have you been pinching again?"

"Isn't it big?"

"I'm trained to see the tiniest details."

"Thanks a lot. It's 1.5 carats."

"You're getting yourself into *serious* trouble."

"Yeah, I know. Not sure what to do about the Sorbonne. I guess you guys can give Jim an alias too? Do I have to be officially married first in order for that to happen? I'd like to tell him what's going on." I was tired of being alone with the details, yet I still feared Jim would kick me to the curb.

"Things aren't that simple Calina. Continue to do as *I* say, and keep your mouth shut." He sounded extra annoyed tonight and bordered on mean.

"My guys saw you looking at some papers in the condo. Looked intense. Any chance you took them?"

"I'm not telling or giving you anything. I suppose you have that place bugged too?"

"Yeah. Heard everything, except the marriage proposal was muffled by the wind. You have an awesome sex life."

"You're a sick fuck."

"Part of the job. Do you think I can concentrate right now? I keep hearing you scream. The other agents that heard the tape call you *Moana*lina."

"I've had enough. Why are you bugging everywhere I go? There are criminals to bug, not me." I got up from my bar stool, but Snow-Cone grabbed my arm and forced me to sit back down. A lady across the bar gave him a dirty look.

"In all seriousness, we need to bust them soon. We've got people on the street, but you're our inside source."

"I'm not giving you any of the other evidence, until I know you're going to keep me safe. And I'm sure these papers have something to do with how the drugs get into New Orleans."

"Bring me the papers, and I'll figure it out."

"They're secure. I want signed documents that you will keep me safe and the specifications. I'll drop the papers off to you before I head to work. Meet me on the streetcar at 3 p.m. The Driver with the nametag Perry P. works tonight. Be sure to get on *his* car. You can bring me the documents to review and sign. No papers for me, no papers for you."

He nodded and our food arrived. I asked for mine to go. Rick G. made me nauseated.

***

Three hours later, I dressed for work. I folded the crumpled papers from the condo and placed them in my backpack. When I opened my door, Beth was standing at it.

"Can you go on a run?"

"Not now, I'll be late for work. Beer tub girls start at 4 p.m."

"You've been slacking lately."

"So, I don't get paid. I have enough money."

"I'm just wondering what's up?"

"Nothing, just busy with this new position."

I ran past her and headed for the streetcar. Rick G. had saved me a seat. He handed me the documents to read, and I read them thoroughly. I was distracted when a guy got up to leave a few stops later. I tilted my head and saw Jim's Coast Guard colleague, Eli. He had short, buzzed hair. *Why would Jim lie and tell me he had long hair too? Maybe Eli had just gotten a haircut?*

I returned to the papers. They stated that the suspicious activity report from the bank was destroyed. I would be placed in witness protection as discussed and receive money for school in addition to living costs for five years. I would give him the condo papers today, but I wrote in that until I saw my new identity and some money, he wouldn't receive the receipts or the managers' logbook.

"You still have to testify."

I didn't say anything. I had another plan because I didn't trust Snow*flake*. I signed the papers. I wanted to get this over with.

I gave him the papers from the condo, and he examined them. "So, what do they mean exactly? Some drug plan of action from Columbia to Mexico to here? Why were they in Jim's uncle's condo?"

We rounded Lee Circle, and I stood up to exit at the next stop. "Well?" I asked as I began to walk down the streetcar steps.

Rick G. stuck his head out of the window. "You already know."

"Huh?" The streetcar doors closed, and I headed to Bourbon Street.

***

My night progressed as normal. Darla was working with me. She had vowed to straighten herself up after her drug overdose, and I would often hear her in her room, singing along with the lyrics to Depeche Mode's *Clean.*

My shift ended at ten p.m., but I decided to have one of Taco's classic Margaritas while I waited for Darla to finish working, so I could accompany her home. I kept wondering all night what Rick G. meant on the streetcar. I was about to find out.

I was sitting at the far corner of the courtyard bar when I saw Jim walk towards the owner's office on the other side of the club. I had forgotten to tell him that I switched shifts with another girl.

I rose to call out to him, but I stopped myself before the words could leave my mouth. In Jim's hands, I saw a single carton of tennis balls that he took out of his backpack. I began to sweat. What I was thinking could not be true. My fiancée could not have been doing the same thing I had done. Or worse.

I followed him to learn more and hid behind a corner near Paul's office. I had to be careful how close I went. Paul's office now had cameras in and around it.

I heard Will ask, "Who was this Foley kid anyway?"

"College kid moving product. Got too big for his britches. Knew he would come around sometime. Figured the no hoodie thing would provoke him into a fight. Didn't expect him to be from a family that would sue." Paul stated.

Was he admitting to attempted murder?

Will spoke again. "I don't think college kids are a good idea to move product anymore. My dad's memory ain't so good, but he told me a college student came into the Whitney Bank branch on Tulane's campus. Said the girl deposited a very large sum of cash and got signaled for a suspicious activity report. Said they were all talking about it for a while. Wondering how the girl got the money. Said that some agent came in asking questions."

Shit. Toscano *was* Will's dad! *And, Rick G. never silenced the bank employees. Asshole.*

"When was this? Why didn't you open your mouth earlier?" Paul reprimanded Will and didn't give him a chance to

242

answer. "See if your Dad can look up the record, and get the person's name. They could be a leak."

Luckily, it was Saturday night and the banks would be closed tomorrow.

Paul continued, "It could be one of Beth's runners like the last punk. Kevin, ask your girlfriend who she has running for her."

"Could be her newest roommate." Kevin responded.

"Who's that?" Paul asked.

Shit again. I tiptoed forward to peak into the office.

"Calina isn't a drug runner." Jim spoke up. He pulled a Ziploc bag of cocaine from a slit in his tennis balls and threw it down on a table where Paul and Kevin sat. Probably a distraction technique for my benefit.

"I have three girl. I don't like carrying this shit around. I'm in acquisitions not distribution. Kevin should have arranged a pickup, especially for personal use."

My boyfriend was in acquisitions?

Kevin responded. "Fuck you. Your last shipment was half the size. Your fingers are supposed to be on the pulse of the sector. You have access to information. Intel. Use it faster."

"I've told you before, the quantities are low due to new methods of clandestine transpo."

Kevin interrupted. "Fancy word."

Jim ignored him. "I've told you another shipment is coming in soon."

Paul placed the drugs under a floorboard. Kevin turned to him. "With the goods low, we should get into boys. Mixing it up can be cheaper."

"Goddamn you, Kevin. No heroin. No way. You just want the fucking nod. I already told you to get off the girl, and you wouldn't have a problem."

I thought back to cab driver George asking for girls and Kevin talking to Paul about boys when I thought he was cheating on Beth. *Girls* were cocaine and *boys* were heroin. Paul had said get off the girl and he wouldn't need the boy. In this case, if he got off the stimulant or coke, he wouldn't need the downer or the heroin. They must have thought they were cool using street slang. Street slang I never learned from Wacky Cracky Jacky. But, she was hardly big time and not smart enough to have code words, however dumb they were.

"Goddamn it, Paul. I don't have a problem. Rich people want it. Dinosaurs."

"I ain't getting into heroin dealing for the middle aged. Tell em to take a fucking Quaalude. They can get em in Mexico-they're making a comeback."

"You're just worried about the bullshit, lower class, negative connotations of it."

"Damn right. No H. You should trust me. I've been like a father to you."

Kevin pointed at Jim. "You're probably just listening to your *real* family. The prodigal nephew."

I felt sick, but tried to stay calm. Everything made sense now, including the papers in the condo. How could I have been so blind not to see all the details? They had masterminded a whole operation. I was an amateur compared to my fiancée. No wonder he constantly told me not to worry about money. Jackson was right. I did have a thick skull, mired in the big picture of cleaning my slate, instead of examining all the people around me and the roles they played.

Kevin decided to continue the attack on Jim. "How do you know your girlfriend ain't running?"

"If she is, Jim will take care of her." Paul answered for him.

Not being able to stand still, I must have moved and made a noise. Paul spotted me first. "Employees aren't allowed up here unless you're a manager."

He had seen me with Jim before. Kissing, sitting on his lap, holding hands.

Jim answered. "Paul, this is my fiancé, Calina. Calina, my uncle Paul."

"New family, huh? Hope she knows it's for love, not money in *this* family. You'll have to sign a pre-nup, honey."

"Knock it off, Paul. Cal, what's wrong?" Jim asked.

"Oh, I, uh, I dropped the back of my earring, and I can't find it on the floor."

"Normally, when someone drops the back of their earring, they grab their ear, not their mouth." Paul stared at me.

I dropped my hand that was pulling at my lippy flesh. Clearly, a nervous reaction. "I'm upset. My birth Mom gave it to me when I was a baby. Forget it, I can find a spare back."

What a dumb conversation, I thought, as I silently agreed with Jim that his uncle was exactly as he had described.

Chapter 19

I had feared Jim, an upstanding Coast Guardsman, would be devastated by his girlfriend's simple drug pinching and would send me packing before I had even moved into his apartment. Now, confused and angry, I still didn't want to believe he could not only be involved, but at the *top* of the drug ring.

In order to get out of Paul's office quickly, I had said I was leaving for the night. Forget accompanying Darla home. I had to get to Rick G. Jim told the men he would walk me out.

We walked in silence until we hit Bourbon Street and Jim said, "Paul can be a real dick."

I chose my words carefully. "Well, I can see I'm not that welcome in the family."

"Calina, he's *not* good family. We're starting our own. Just you and me. Trust me."

Trust? I was already mired in lies. How could this charming guy be a drug trafficker, kingpin, whatever he was. Why did he make me fall in love with him just to break my heart? My silence betrayed me.

"You're really upset."

"I just don't understand why you didn't tell me the owner of Black Sevens was your uncle?"

Jim reiterated. "I told you he's no good. That's the truth."

How could I believe anything he said? Jim and tennis balls flashed in my mind. *Wait. Did he know about me?* He had found tennis balls under my sink and questioned me about them. Did he know that *I* had done what he had, but on a much smaller scale? Did he know I was working for Beth? He had said no to the men.

Maybe he just wanted to steal the special edition balls for his own purposes. I still loved him, despite his guilt. And how could I be angry with him when I was in on the operation? I wanted to tell him the clock was ticking on our relationship, and Rick G. planned to bust him and take everything away from us. I didn't want that to happen.

***

Thirty minutes later, I banged on the door. Rick G.'s outside light turned on and a Pit Bull one yard over barked. He opened the door and rubbed his eyes.

"Are you booty calling me? Coasty not giving you enough?"

"Shut up. We need to talk."

"You never silenced the bank employees. Now Paul has ordered Will Toscano to find out from his Bank Teller father who the college student is that deposited a large sum of money. I'm toast. I probably have forty-eight hours since banks are closed on Sundays."

"This will be over before he can find your name."

"Bullshit. I want those papers I gave you back."

"Too late. They are now property of the U.S. Government's case against Paul Jansen and crew. No pun intended."

"My fiancé doesn't work on a boat. He knows when they come in and out."

"Exactly."

"You set me up. This is entrapment or something. You failed to tell me Jim was somehow involved, so I would inadvertently give you information on him."

"Somehow? He's the brilliant mastermind. I gave you a few little hints. You missed a couple of steps on your scavenger list."

"You think this is a fucking game? I'm sorry my acumen failed to help me realize you were playing me. Are you trying to ruin my life?"

"Calina, your boyfriend, fiancée, whatever, is going to go down with or without you. We could have gone into the condo and found those papers. You just brought them to us faster. Let me show you how deep your fiancé is in."

***

Rick G. drove us to the docks. We sat in his car and waited. "You're about to see how the white powder gets into New Orleans. And, how your perfect man is involved. I have photographs, but I felt live in person will make you believe me."

I scowled at him. He looked at his watch and told me, "another minute." After a few went by, Rick G. told me they must be late. At twelve thirty a.m., a large fishing vessel tied its ropes to the dock.

Jim appeared from a building labeled Clancy's Fish Co. and headed for the docks. He looked rugged and convincingly like a dockworker with a dirty uniform. He approached a boat.

The men on board the boat lifted some crates onto the dock. Then, with Jim leading the way, they carried the crates around the corner back to Clancy's Fish Co.

"So they are dropping fish Snow-Cone. Big deal."

"They hide them in the fish holds of those vessels." Rick G. motioned for me to get out of the car. The show was far from over.

I didn't argue with him, for a change, and followed him to the side of the building. He pointed to the back of the building where I should look to, "see the next step."

I did as instructed and saw Jim open the crate. I jumped back as rattlesnakes hissed at him.

A man standing next to him told him to, "Just do it. Do it man." Jim took a large knife and chopped off the heads of the snakes.

"I'm going to be sick." *Twice in one night.*

"Turn back around." Rick G. nudged me. "You'll miss the festivities."

I saw Jim take out plastic vials full of white powder. *This is how the drugs got into the city.*

"The test tubes obviously don't dissolve in the body of the snake. Clever huh?"

Yeah, real, I thought. The fact that Black Sevens used them for alcohol *and* cocaine made me feel my own University chemistry classes hadn't taught me *nearly* enough. I was learning far more lessons outside of school.

I remembered the night I met Jim at Black Sevens for the first time. Will had told him not to hang out there so much. The night of Beth's New Years' Eve Party, he talked to Kevin about, "fishing." He drove a BMW and spent money on fancy dinners. I remembered him talking to Will about, "dry spells." He told Kevin he was in acquisitions not distribution. It all made sense. Especially the, "clandestine transpo," and the, "high season." And, the long hair. *Yeah right he worked in an office.* Was he even *in* the Coast Guard?

I wished I had realized Rick G.'s warning when he looked at my ring and told me I was getting myself into big trouble.

However, Rick G. should not have been hiding this pertinent information from me. *Asshole.*

"Let's go." This time, I instructed Rick G.

As we walked to the car, I thought about how the guy who was supposed to be the love of my life could turn out to be such a criminal? How could my judgment have been so clouded? I contemplated running away and hiding like the good old days when I ran away from my evil foster father Arnie. But I knew I couldn't last too long in a tree house. There had to be a way to work everything out.

Jim would not only never speak to me again, he would kill me when he found out I spied on the operation. I felt I hardly knew the felon I had just spent the last four months with. And although I felt betrayed and lied to, I couldn't change my feelings for him. I had done something illegal too, even if it was on a smaller scale. I still wanted to warn him, and I still wanted to marry him.

Maybe I should tell him to escape to another country, and I would join him later when I disappeared and entered the witness protection program. It could happen? Right? But then there was the possibility that he could be caught first and go straight to jail. Life was not a Monopoly board game. I doubted a get out of jail free card would magically appear in his deck.

I was quiet in the car and for once, Rick G. didn't provoke me to engage him in any witty banter. Why was the institution always trying to fuck me over? The childcare system, school, the U.S. government? I was finished with all this bullshit. It was time for me to take matters into my own hands.

"I can't testify against them."

"You have to. Think about the good you are doing. Accept what's real and move on. It'll be better for everyone. Just please don't blow your cover with your boyfriend."

"You didn't tell me my own boyfriend was involved before I signed your papers. These guys, Kevin, all the other people involved, my *own* boyfriend, they'll come after me as soon as they're free from prison. And you tell me to think about the good. Fuck you."

I could see I wasn't going to get anywhere with Rick G.

"You signed an agreement."

"I want a new one."

"It doesn't work like that."

But it did for me. A piece of paper couldn't protect my life.

***

I called my old party partner at one a.m., and by one-thirty a.m. we headed back down to the French Quarter. I needed to drown my confusion and sorrow the old fashioned college way: drinking. Bourbon Street called our name like a whispering little devil on one side of the head. Of course, we wouldn't go near

Black Sevens. We had frozen strawberry Margaritas at Pat O'Brien's and then headed to dance at OZ where we knew no annoying guys would hit on us since it was on the gay block of Bourbon Street.

Next, we went back down to Cat's Meow to make fun of the drunk people singing Karaoke. An underage teenage girl named Britney from Kentwood was singing on the stage. She looked familiar from my days spent in that small town. She wore her hair in braids and must have been practicing some routine. Someone announced her first album and music video was about to come out and it confirmed my assessment.

A guy came up to me and wanted to dance, but I just wanted to party with Jackson and be left alone. I displayed my hand, and he got the hint by walking away. "Are you sure you want to get married?" Jackson asked.

"Not anymore." Uh-oh. The alcohol was talking.

"I never thought I would hear you say that. What's going on?"

"Just some trouble. I don't want to talk about it right now."

"Is it the same thing you couldn't tell me when you left before watching *Dumbo*?"

"Yeah."

"By the way. Everyone should watch stoned *Dumbo*."

"You mean *Dumbo* stoned?"

"Exactly."

A skinny black man approached us. "Why does that guy have a comb stuck in his hair?" Jackson surprisingly used tact and whispered her question to me. It was too late to answer. "Hey ladies, want to smoke some weed?"

"Sure." Jackson thought she answered for the both of us.

"Don't touch that weed Jackson. He could be a narcotics cop trying to entrap us."

"Girl, you crazy." The short thug replied. "Here." He handed Jackson weed and walked away.

"Thanks for going ape shit on his ass, Calina. Now we have weed and nothing to smoke it out of."

"You never know."

Jackson led me out of the club. "Let's go to my namesake square and buy a bowl."

"I'm not going down there at night. All the freaks come out."

"They're out all day."

"Well, the dangerous ones."

We walked down Bourbon Street and a skinny black man wearing a torn shirt stopped us with a box full of trinkets. "Got anything to smoke out of?" Jackson asked.

He handed her a clear, cracked tube. She gave him ten dollars. After the exchange, I asked, "You're going to smoke weed out of a crack pipe?"

"Whatever works after your paranoia back there. Wait, that's what this thing has to do with, doesn't it? You're in some kind of *drug* trouble, aren't you? You got caught. Holy shit. You better tell me everything."

"Stop being so expressive. I never know who's watching."

Chapter 20

Later that night, Jackson drove me in her new Z3 BMW to meet Lidell from Slidell. She thought her new ride went with our covert plan. I wasn't going to let the establishment screw me. It's a clever word, isn't it? That establishment. Stands for so many things. It's a failure in my eyes.

I had told Jackson everything. I was tired of being alone with my secrets, and I needed help. Rick G. wasn't gonna cut it. Jackson called a family friend supposedly in the DEA. *Above* Rick G.

We arrived at a Popeyes in Slidell. Lidell had the 4 a.m. shift.

"You know how to use this, girl?" He asked as he handed me a Glock, and I gave him an envelope with cash.

"Foster father number 6."

"Damn girl, that system ain't so bad."

"Listen Lidell, you're not going to want to do any runs anytime soon. Trust me on this one."

"No worries. I got a lot of cash saved. Think I might retire to Natchitoches. You want a fried crawfish breakfast biscuit?"

Lidell from Slidell was smarter than I thought.

I finally went to bed at five a.m. My pillow and sheets smelled like Jim. If we were separated, eventually the smell would fade, and I would be left with nothing.

I woke at one p.m. on Sunday. Jim called at three p.m. and reminded me I was supposed to move in with him that night. He didn't want me to go to work. It was time to quit Black Sevens, and he would tell Will I wasn't coming in. I refused. I couldn't tell him why I had to go in again one more time, and he didn't give me a valid reason why *not* to. Besides, it was now or never for me. The clock was ticking.

I arrived at Jackson's dorm at eight p.m. in a cab. The streetcar was too public for her, although if she only knew how many people sat in these cab seats, she might rethink her decision. The Glock and an external hard drive were in my book bag.

Ashley the ho, Shelia the computer wiz, Mindy the bitch, and Marni the druggie came along. It's nice to have all kinds of stereotypical friends in college. Pedro also came along as the male figure, just in case we needed some muscle.

Bob the cab driver, began to entertain us for the drive. "I once drove a teacher down to Bourbon Street. She was from Oklahoma. I told her to ask her school kids at what temperature does Fahrenheit meet Celsius. She said that was a great idea to see if the kids were motivated to find out."

"I didn't know cab drivers were teaching the kids of America." Jackson replied.

I nudged her. She could be so embarrassing sometimes, and I felt compelled to stick up for the cabbie. "My boyfriend told me cab drivers do quite well. Some make over one grand a week."

"Maybe if your boyfriend wasn't so into acquiring money, we wouldn't be on our way…"

I cut her off. "Not everyone is born into wealth, Jackson."

Marni chimed in. "That justifies a life of crime."

Ashley asked, "Tell me again-why are we going to Black Sevens? That place is tourist cheese."

Jackson answered, "Just stick to the plan like we told you. Flirt when we say flirt."

"Remember the buzzer to the door is under the desk." I whispered to them. "And remember, you *must* disable the camera in the office before you start."

We stepped onto Bourbon Street five minutes later. I reiterated to Jackson that she *must* come into the club at ten, when it got busy. Until that time, she would hang out at the Maison Dupuy on Toulouse Street, two blocks away from Bourbon Street.

She would serve as the leader, but she wouldn't have it any other way, anyway. They would return to the Maison Dupuy after my plan was completed. Her parents always stayed there, and the hotel had installed Internet for their room. This was *key* for us.

In the coming years, technology would change so much. The whole notion of stealing or getting video footage would be so much easier. People could just hit record on their cell phones the minute anything happened.

"Remember, the video footage is just as important as the logbooks and receipts. It shows all of them partaking in manipulating the registers. This way, I won't have to testify for that loony agent. I'll tell him I have information for him, but first I want to leave and be protected and then he will receive word where the fo is."

"The what?"

"Information."

"Okay, wanna-be-ghetto girl."

"Learned it from a White Wanna-Be Rapper. You told the girls what to do, right?"

"Affirmative chief. Like your intonation."

"I need to get out of this mess."

"Yeah, but witness protection? And what about Jim? How are you going to say goodbye to that felon?"

"One thing at a time." The truth was, I had no idea how all of this would end. I parted from Jackson and crew.

Sunday night wasn't the busiest night in the club, however it was Jazz Fest, so the city was flooded with visitors. The last weekend in April and the first weekend in May, a big festival of music was held at the New Orleans Fair Grounds, a thoroughbred racetrack.

Before I got to Black Sevens, I made a stop to see if Beth was at Dick's Palace. I hadn't seen her last night, and I was afraid of *what* she had told Kevin and crew. I also had to give her the keys to 588 Walnut Street.

When I entered Dick's, I heard Kraftwerk playing. The techno beats droned on for two minutes before a voice said, "Tour de France." Who thought of that song? Did someone sit down and think, lets make some techno beats and throw in some words here and there? How is that creative? Although it did catapult them into one hit wonder status.

I saw that Beth was dancing and figured I would talk to her tomorrow instead. When the rotating spotlight stopped on her, I saw a black bruise on her arm. No doubt courtesy of Kevin. She had obviously tried to cover it up. A foster child knows that no amount of makeup can cover up a bad fight. It might conceal it a little in the day, but at night, in the spotlight, it just looks all pasty.

I left Dick's and headed to Black Sevens. When I entered the club, I spotted Darla prancing around. She should have worked at Dick's Palace.

I went upstairs to check in and said hello to Will. "How ya doing?" He spoke to his papers. He was never rude to me. *Did he know something? Were they on to me?* Maybe he was just having a bad day. Or, maybe after Jim and I left last night, they had found out something more. I needed to be careful.

Downstairs, Darla approached me. "We aren't going to take in a new roommate. At this point, we feel it would be another huge liability."

Liability for who? I had paid Beth back all the money she had ever fronted me. I shivered, thinking about what had happened to their last roommate. Had Toscano found my name already, or had Beth told Kevin I was a runner? Why would they tell Darla, the loose cannon, anything?

A customer asked for a shot, and I moved away from Darla. Jackson and entourage entered on schedule and by eleven p.m., the girls had successfully charmed Round Randy and Will. Put a nice piece of ass in front of these guys and you had the power.

Paul had left the club like he did every night. Jackson was working her magic dropping tons of money buying people drinks. She had never been to Black Sevens before. As much as she was a party girl, she just stuck to her favorite places and her parents chain club.

When Round Randy had to return upstairs, the plan began to develop.

"Oh, show me your office. I love offices." Ashley proclaimed to Round Randy, as I handed them shots, and they kept telling me I was the best cocktail waitress *ever. Damn straight.*

"We don't let customers upstairs." Round Randy screeched.

I heard Will whisper to Round Randy. "That's Jackson Milton and her friends. She's spending tons of dough."

Round Randy looked at him expressionless.

"You know, the Miltons of the Forever Club. That's her Daddy's club."

"Well then, coupla minutes won't hurt nobody." *Little did he know,* I thought.

The three girls followed Round Randy upstairs. I wanted to be there too, in case anything went wrong. As planned, the girls had just finished my shot tray, and I needed to follow Round Randy upstairs so he could give me another. The girls had passed the shots out to partiers in the club, so they wouldn't get drunk. However, they were so watered down, I wasn't worried about their sobriety.

As soon as they entered the office, Shelia's eyes darted around the office to find the power source for the office camera. Ashley was already going to work, sitting on Round Randy's fat ass lap. "Have some of my drink, Randy." She put the cup up to his lips and he tilted his head back. Mindy massaged his neck, but not without cringing behind his back and looking to Ashley for the next step. Shelia was able to stand nearby and, "accidentally," unplug the camera.

"Why you still up here Calina? Get lost. You're a big mouth. Might say I raped someone."

Everyone was acting weird tonight. They had to be on to me. Round Randy was mean, but had never said anything like that to me before. I walked into the next room and stood there for a moment. I was worried if I didn't go back down soon, Will would notice, but I wanted to make sure the plan went down.

"More drinky drink." I heard Ashley say. Then after another minute, I heard Marni say, "Thank god. I thought Michael might have given me a bad batch. I had to double roofie the fat fuck."

I peaked my head in. Shelia had gone to work on the computer system. "Calina, go back down. We got this."

Marni told me, "I didn't get fucked up tonight on purpose. I feel like I'm taking a test, but this one I want to pass." She pointed at her work of art, a passed out, snoring Round Randy.

The plan was to get the IP address, username and password to the server that housed all the security videos. Then, we could access the server from Maison Dupuy, download and record the videos and save them to an external hard drive.

I went back downstairs as instructed. Jackson and Mindy were still charming Will. They didn't ask me for shots because they knew if I sold the tray too fast, I would have to return upstairs and since Round Randy locked the fridge, I would have no way to replenish them. Our physical backup, Pedro, sat at Taco's bar eyeing the crowd and making sure the girls were okay.

At the end of fifteen minutes, Jackson called, "Barmaid." I hated that word, but had to remember it was part of the plan. I walked over to her and she exclaimed, "More shots for everyone!" My shots were depleted, and I returned upstairs to check on the girls with my excuse of getting another tray.

Back upstairs, Shelia told me, "Give me one more minute."

I was nervous. "Do you think it's working?"

"Shelia's smarter than all the professors!" Mindy reminded me.

I nodded and heard Will's voice. "How's the party up there?"

"Shit." I whispered. "Hurry."

"We're coming up to join you!" Jackson hollered. I knew her well enough to know that she never got nervous. The only time she had, was when her father called to lecture her that she must *actually* graduate for her inheritance, and now I could hear the same quiver in her voice.

"Done." Shelia whispered and jumped up to plug the video camera back in. We all turned to the doorway with blank expressions on our faces.

Will stood in the doorway with Jackson who mouthed, "I tried to stop him."

Now it was my turn to lead. "Something's wrong with Randy. I tried to revive him, but he's out cold."

"Son of a bitch probably overdosed on something. Cold medication, most likely. He's got some nose problem."

"That wouldn't be cold medication." Jackson interjected, and I gave her the wide-eyed, 'shut up,' look.

"No, like some medical thing. Shit. I gotta be on the floor. Let me call Paul. Now maybe he'll see why I'm a better option to run this place. You girls go back downstairs and have fun. Not you, Calina. You need another tray, and you're working until six a.m."

Oh shit. Will never made me take another tray out at the end of the night like Round Randy. The girls looked at me. This wasn't part of the plan. They began to walk downstairs.

A minute later, I went back downstairs with a new tray and found the girls to tell them to go back to the hotel. I would meet them after six a.m. Darla said in passing, "You definitely hog everything for yourself, Calina."

This time, I knew she was referring to the, "wealthy customers," or *my* friends, but I knew she was also alluding to something more.

"They're on to me. Everyone's been really weird and Beth has a huge bruise." I whispered to Jackson and Pedro.

266

Pedro responded, "You're coming with us, Calina. It's time to walk away. It doesn't take a Shelia to figure out something is up."

He was right. Something *was* up and there was nothing left for me to do at Black Sevens. I laid down my tray and went to get my bag. When I arrived upstairs, Will came out of the office and asked why people were taking shots from my tray. "I quit. It's been real."

I practically sprinted out of the club, careful not to pass by Meyers or Donovan who were back after their murder sabbatical. They could be ordered to grab and suffocate me at any moment. They were set to go to court soon. The toxicology report came back. Yes, James Foley was over the legal limit, but intoxication *and suffocation* were the cause of death.

When I got to the room at Maison Dupuy, Marni told us we should break out a bottle of champagne, as she held the managers' logbook in the air. "Stashed it in my purse."

"You're the best. What about the register receipts?"

Mindy took them out of her Kate Spade bag.

"We haven't seen if the main event worked yet." Ashley cautioned.

Shelia started to hook up her laptop. "Are you doubting me? I broke into the computer system and did your Information Systems exam."

Ashley nodded in remembrance.

Jackson chimed in. "My parents didn't really get why I needed a laptop. Made a BS excuse about studying off campus."

"Besides its BS, Bourbon Street *does* have educational value." Pedro stated.

"We don't have much time. When Paul realizes the cameras in the office were turned off, he might be on to us and disconnect the server." We probably had a little bit more time than I intimated. Paul was most likely out on the town and not sitting at home watching his club. I had seen him out partying on more than one occasion. He liked chic places like The W Hotel bar and The Red Room.

Shelia explained that after we logged onto their server, we could download video and save it on an external hard drive. We had to pick the most important footage because the external hard-drive had a limited capacity for large video files. "Welcome to surveillance on your desktop. It looks like the footage is in different folders corresponding to camera numbers and dates. Any preferences on what to open, Calina?"

I definitely wanted to record the footage with the register manipulation so we found the cameras over the registers and the times when I knew the managers changed over the registers.

Of course, we also got the footage from Paul's office from the night I was present for his murder confession. The last clip I wanted was *after* I left Paul's office. I wanted to see if anything else went down.

Sure enough, we saw Beth on screen, sitting in the office with Will, Round Randy, Paul and Kevin. Everyone but Jim. Who as I knew now, had gone to the docks to get more drugs or run his acquisitions.

On screen, Beth admitted, "She was running drugs for me, but she's harmless."

"You betrayed all of us by bringing her in." Kevin smacked Beth hard and we all gasped at the footage as she fell to the floor, and he kicked her arm. Now I knew for sure where her bruise came from, not that I doubted Kevin was the culprit.

Paul said, "We'll just take care a her like your old roommate." Everyone gasped. The Internet feed went wavy.

"Why does it pause like that?" Jackson asked.

"Slow technology." Shelia explained. "It's called "buffering."

The feed came back on. "I'm not letting that twit ruin everything. I'll go after her. Shut her up permanently." Kevin said. We all gasped again and all the girls looked at me as I stared straight ahead at the screen.

Round Randy spoke next, "If she's given the DEA information, they'll give it to the IRS. Then every single manager receiving a cash bonus from the illegal money will go to jail."

Paul was harsh as he shouted back at Round Randy. "You fat fuck, I don't need you to tell me how this could all be ruined."

Off screen, Jackson mumbled, "Nice future in-law."

Back on screen, Kevin said to Paul, "I told Jim he shouldn't have been hanging out with that twit."

"You're ruining everything yourself you drug addict." Beth interjected, and I thought she was probably just angry with him, more than she was sticking up for me.

"The drugs were better than the fuck every time!" Kevin hit her again, and she screamed.

"What if the DEA snaps a picture of her and Jim together?" Round Randy asked.

"She's not an actor, and the DEA ain't the paparazzi. Get real." Will replied.

"Jim will do whatever I say. When I took him in, I trained him to be just like me. Business before heart. Always. I'll have him dispose of her quickly and quietly." Paul stated. "If she has been a leak, she will be silenced." The feed went dead. Now, on tape, I had two attempted murder confessions.

Chapter 21

"Settle down Betty Ford."

Jackson took the champagne out of my hand. I hadn't wanted it, since semantically it indicated happy occasions, but it *was* the only thing around, and I needed a drink. The girls and reluctantly, Pedro, had left the hotel shortly after our discovery.

"Jim wanted to talk and told me not to go to work, but I wouldn't listen."

"If you had, you could be six feet under right now."

"I'm so confused by everything that's happened in the past four months. I went from college student to...to...."

"Illegal Perry Mason!"

"A criminal defense lawyer? That doesn't make sense. And what does that make you? Della Street?" I couldn't believe Jackson knew of a show that came out decades before her time. Maybe it was the revival in the 80s.

"My grandparents are friends with Barbara Hale, so maybe by association." That explained her knowledge.

We heard a knock at the door. I put my hand to my lips, fearful she would trip up and ask who was at the door.

"Calina, it's Beth. Open up. We need to talk, sweetie."
Yeah right. *Pretending* to be on my side. I motioned for Jackson
to follow me to the sliding glass door, and we stepped onto the
balcony. Thank god we were only on the second floor.

"Shit, Will must have searched every hotel under your
parent's name. We need to leave here right away."

"What? I paid for the room."

"Since when have you cared about two hundred bucks?"

I began to climb over the balcony, ready to fall onto the one
below. My flexibility from kickboxing would really have to kick
in now. *Pun intended.*

"Take off your heels." I ordered Jackson, who was hesitant
to move.

"These are six-hundred-dollar Jimmy Choos!"

We heard pounding at the door. Beth had gotten angry,
very fast. Then we heard Kevin's voice. "You fucking twit. Open
the goddamn door."

"Choo rhymes with poo. Take them off now or die by the
hand of a psycho."

Seconds later, Jackson held my hand in one of hers while
her shoes dangled in the other. She watched in horror as they
dropped into a puddle of stale vomit and beer on Bourbon Street.

We ran down Toulouse Street and onto Royal Street, the
street parallel to Bourbon. No amount of Milton money could pay

for my joy in seeing Jackson Milton running through the dirty streets of New Orleans barefoot.

When Kevin and Beth got into our hotel room, they would find the laptop we left behind. *And,* a bible.

***

On Royal Street, we tried to hail a flag with no success. Sometimes, it's damn near impossible. People either hail it first, or it drives right by you on its way to pick up someone who already called via telephone. That's why after work we went down to the cabstand at The Royal Senesta where you could ring the bell and it would magically call the cab for you. Sometimes that was even slow or no one came.

"What should we do?" I asked Jackson. I was out of ideas.

"Well, the earliest my friend can meet us is at five p.m. tomorrow. He said he would take the first flight out."

Jackson referred to her family friend high up in the DEA that she had called. Her parents had met him when he first started as a field agent back in the 80s. He helped them when some Italians from New York tried to extort one of their clubs and force them to launder money. I would later meet a distant relative from that same family in a graduate school program. Life really is one degree of separation.

We kept walking, not very fast, but faster than we would have, had Jackson been wearing her heels. We were headed back to Canal Street and in the direction back to uptown. "We've got to hide out somewhere. Somewhere Kevin can't find us."

It was midnight and the quarter was still crowded. It wasn't body to body in terms of space, like at Mardi Gras time, but there was a lot of partying going on due to Jazz Fest. However, there weren't enough bodies to keep me from spotting Kevin.

"Shit. Follow me." We ducked and quickly blended into the crowd, but luck was *not* on my side because on the next street, a van abruptly pulled up and stopped next to us. Jim jumped out and grabbed a hold of me, shoving me into the van. An unknown man grabbed Jackson and did the same.

Inside the van, I struggled. Jim was stronger than I thought.

"Calina, stop. It's okay." He told me.

"If you're going to put a bullet in my head, just do it fast. You know I don't like anticipation." I reached for my backpack to get my own Glock. I pulled it out and tried to point it as Jim went to grab my wrist.

"Calina, this is Agent Porter." Jackson screamed.

"Your family friend?"

"Yes."

I looked at Jim and at Agent Porter.

"What's going on here? Why are you with him?" I asked Jim.

Agent Porter spoke. "I've been doing my own investigation the past few hours. I'm sorry I had such an incompetent agent on the job. DEA Agent Rick Grant made some major errors in "Coked Up 7's.""

"Coked up what a?"

Jim turned to Agent Porter. "I told you the name was dumb."

Porter ignored him and continued, "The different law enforcement agencies- the DEA, FBI, Coast Guard- all have interagency agreements to work together. In this case, they've been grossly ignored. Agent Grant didn't check to see *who* was working *what*. *These* kinds of things are becoming all too commonplace, unfortunately."

"So this means you..." I turned to Jim.

"I'm CGIS-Coast Guard Investigative Services. When I moved back to New Orleans, I knew my uncle was scamming and selling drugs. I came up with the plan to set Black Sevens up.

My uncle thinks I'm a yeoman. My rank is really first class petty officer. The other guys, Eli and Josh, thought I was a yeoman on Temporary Assigned Duty. Posing as a yeoman in the office enabled me to filter information. Since I'm at the pulse of the intel, I could find out about suspect vessels and allow illegal activity in, by steering away the Coast Guard that would normally make a bust. All for the purpose of taking down Paul Jansen's ring."

"Why didn't you tell me?" I asked.

"I'm sorry, Calina. I couldn't. It was *strictly,* "need to know." It would have put you and the whole operation in jeopardy. The only one who knew about me was the head of the Coast Guard, and now Porter, *head* of the DEA. I realized someone else was on to them when I found out about you. Obviously Rick Grant didn't know about me."

"So you know all about me?"

"You hid it well. In the beginning your ignorance tipped me off that you were innocent. I even had you ride with cab driver George just to see what you knew. Later, I suspected you when I found the tennis balls in your bathroom. But I didn't really know until last night when Will Toscano mentioned the bank drop. I did my research and found out about the DEA involvement and that led me to call Porter. Then, Beth finally confirmed you were running and my uncle told me to take care of you."

Porter said, "Rick Grant should have checked with special assignments. It's sad how it's going to take a huge disaster to get all the agencies to cooperate and work with one another in a more informed manner." *And a few years later, that was 9-11.*

"I'm sorry I didn't tell you what was going on." I told Jim.

"It's okay. I know what kind of bastards you worked for. And we all know what happened to Beth Bloom's last roommate. I didn't want that to happen to you."

There was an awkward moment, as we had the audience of Jackson and Agent Porter. Porter broke the silence.

"We're set to bust them at two a.m. when a shipment will come in from the docks, and the drop will be made to Black Sevens. I still need all of your evidence, Calina. I know you are on the right side. I'm aware of your troubles, and you'll be completely exonerated."

"I'll be running for the rest of my life from those creeps."

"Calina, if everything goes as planned and we nab Kevin and crew, you will be well rewarded. You have my word."

"But I had Rick Grant's word and look where that led me."

"From what Jackson tells me, you have demonstrated remarkable spirit and initiative. Again, you have my word you will be protected." Porter said.

"I need to know my *new* demands are met and that I'm protected. Then I will tell you where *all* of the evidence is."

Porter asked, "what were your *old* demands?"

"I see Snow-Cone definitely didn't know how to rap.

They all looked at me oddly. Except for Jackson.

Chapter 22

Jim was dropped off at the docks by the van, and Porter took Jackson and I to a local DEA office before going to bust the club. Agent Rick G., aka Snow Cone, would still be assisting despite his colossal screw up. Before the director left, he took me into a room alone and asked, "Have you come to a decision to submit your evidence?"

"They'll know it was me. I can't live in witness protection. The social workers had good intentions, but even they couldn't protect me. The institution has let me down so many times. I can't let it screw me a final time. I can see my obituary reading, 'untimely death due to bizarre circumstances.'"

"What if there was another way, Calina?"

"What other way?"

"Have you ever heard of Frank Abagnale Jr.?"

I shook my head no.

"He was a con artist that passed millions of dollars worth of bad checks. He consults for the federal government now on embezzlement cases. He's come up with fraud prevention programs." In 2002, they would make a movie about the guy starring Leonardo DiCaprio.

"You're offering me a job?"

"We're offering to allow you to finish your schooling free of charge and train to be with us. We think you will enjoy your career. Who needs to be a doctor? You were struggling with those sciences anyway." He gave me a few more details and told me to think about it before he left.

I joined Jackson back in the lounge where we helped ourselves to coffee. "I don't know if I can believe Porter's promises. I've always had to protect myself, Jackson. He doesn't get that I don't trust anyone, even the highest of authority."

"He's a good guy, Calina."

"Your parents are rich. I'm just a poor girl. The system doesn't care about me. I can't do anything for anyone after this."

"Porter's not gonna screw you, Calina. You can give the evidence you worked hard for and put away these sleaze bags who threatened your life. You'll take down a major crime ring in this city. We'll celebrate later at Balcony Bar."

"How are you even thinking of partying right now? Aren't you tired from all I've put you through?"

"You know me. If there's partying to be done, I'm wide awake."

Wouldn't the Director be pleased to know that in the past, Jackson had also contributed to the illegal flow and payout at Black Sevens.

I loved New Orleans and would deeply miss it. Porter wanted me at Georgetown. He told me he knew I was smart, and had just gotten a little misled along the way, seeing as I had a chaotic life.

"He wants me to leave tomorrow and go live with his family for the summer and get acquainted with the area. Prove to me that I'll be safe. He has a daughter my age."

"Yeah, she's okay. A well behaved girl. She'll keep you out of trouble."

"I can't count on her to learn the new bar scene?"

"Not unless you consider the Tea Express Café your next Black Sevens."

"I guess I *do* need to take some time off from the bar scene."

"We'll take turns visiting. Wait, what are you going to do about Jim?"

"I don't know." I hadn't had time to think. My exhaustion and the thought of facing another decision made me upset. "My whole life, all I wanted was a family, to feel loved, protected. I felt so protected with him, until I thought he was guilty."

"Did you? Because you seemed pretty alone with your guilt until you told me about Black Sevens. For a smart girl, you're as blind as an old dog."

Oh no. I felt her words of wisdom were going to confuse me more, but then she said the most profound thing. "You've been taking care of yourself your whole life. A damn good job of it. Sometimes when we're upset over what we lose, or think we've lost, we forget to look at what we have. We forget to look at ourselves."

Jackson was more astute than she had ever been in the classroom. Every time throughout my life that I had awoken from a nightmare, sweaty, my heart racing, wanting someone to save me from difficult life situations, I now realized that I had done it myself.

"You're so independent. I know you want a family, but you have your whole life. I know it looks like I had it all. Great parents shelling out money whenever I wanted, but how many times were they off at some exotic location without the kids?

Honestly, you've been more like family to me than my own. I know we've had our differences at times, but I want you to know that." She gave me a big hug, and we reminisced about all our fun times the past two years until the director came back hours later.

He told her to go back to her dorm and to get some sleep. I said goodbye, almost ready to take my first plane ride.

Agent Porter escorted me to a main room where many uniformed men sat at desks. He explained that the jail cells were in the back. Once seated, he told me, "Everything went well.

Kevin is currently in a cell. They arrested Darla twenty minutes ago when she came to visit and stuck a thin straw through the holes of the visitor box in order to blow coke through her boyfriend's nose."

"What a dedicated couple. Guess they *were* having a thing. His girlfriend is actually Beth Bloom."

"Ah, Celexa on the street. I guess she was having her fun on the side. We caught her with Will Toscano in the walk in cooler out back."

"Keeping the jello shots company, I see."

"She'll be arriving shortly."

"Through here? I need to leave."

"It's okay. Trust me."

A minute later, some cops entered with a handcuffed Beth, who spotted me. "She screamed, "I really thought you were a poor college student. You should receive an Academy Award."

The cops told Beth to, "come on," and carted her away. Director Porter then told me, "I know you were nervous about them coming after you. I decided that if they thought you were an agent posing as a student, then you wouldn't have to enter witness protection. This way, they think you just infiltrated rather than betrayed them."

"The evidence is in room 22 of the Maison Dupuy. Ignore the do not disturb sign on the door. I cut a hole in the mattress and put the managers' logbooks and receipts there. Those bathroom sewing kits finally came in handy."

I was convinced Porter had better bargaining power than SnowCone.

***

After the bust, I went to Jim's apartment. I had a key, but with everything that had just happened, I decided to knock. He opened the door, smiled and motioned for me to come in. Knowing the truth, I wanted to hug him, but I sat across from him, frozen.

The only thing I ever really wanted was to belong. I wanted to experience the feeling of someone wondering where I had been, what I had seen, what I had done. I wanted to create a community of people that lasted for more than a year. People, that, years later, looked back and reminisced. I thought going to a University was my chance. I thought my worth was through having a family and if I couldn't belong, I wanted to be someone else. To be in their head and see their dreams, feel their movements instead of my own, like an out of body experience. I didn't anymore. I was comfortable in my own skin.

Jim started the conversation. "I was angry at the institution when my family died. I thought it should have protected me. My mother and brother were killed just because they were with my father the day he had to go to court to testify against a local drug kingpin bringing drugs in for a Columbian cartel."

"Medellin cartel?" I asked, thinking back to my education that night at the diner with Taco.

"I'm impressed. Actually, the Cali Cartel, Medellin's competition at the time, so to speak. Anyway, I was sick that day, at my Grandparents house. I thought the city and the federal government should have protected me. My uncle is rotten to the core. I didn't want to live with him. I blamed the institution for years. Tried to rebel. I lied, I cheat, I stole. A boy needs his father."

"A girl needs her mother."

"We're chaos with chaos."

I sat beside him on the couch. "In one foster family, we used to shop at Safeway cause my foster father said they had the best meat to steal. I fended for myself all my life, and college was my ticket to a real job one day, not a store clerk or a waitress. I got hit, I got thrown in juvie two times. Once because they thought an eight-year-old was a drug ring mastermind, the other for fighting back when I got picked on. I wanted to lift the shadow that's been on me my whole life. It wasn't like I was going to make a career of running drugs. I did it to get back into school. And I think I've certainly reformed myself by helping spy."

"You helped very well. Heard you got some of the same things I collected. And nice job with that manager's log. Don't know how I would have gotten the information that I did, if I hadn't falsely been on the inside. You should learn to let go of the past though. But because of mine, I understand yours and all that you did."

"How did you finally forgive?"

"Years of therapy and deciding I wanted to help other people in some way. Keep people safe. All the times I picked you up from work, I thought I was doing a good job, but I failed."

"So I was a charity case?"

"No. I love you, and I wanted to see that you were protected from them."

"Then you should have told me what was going on from the beginning! That you were on temporary assigned duty."

"Remember, the other Coast Guards in that office thought I was a yeoman on temporary assigned duty posing as a fisherman to make sure proper docking protocol was initiated. My rank is First Class Petty Officer, and I'm CGIS. Not many people are in the need to know when I'm on a special assignment. It would jeopardize everything. That's why only the head of the Coast Guard knew and now Porter. The need to know is *that* limited."

"So you thought I would be a leak? Sounds like your job comes first."

"It's not like that, Calina. It's for your protection."

"So you busted your own uncle." I said in contemplation.

"You know how family sometimes doesn't act like family. You were around enough bad ones. I told you the truth about him.

285

He squandered what was left to me and was verbally and physically abusive. He didn't give any of my money back even after he made his first honest bucks from Black Sevens. Always told me I wouldn't amount to anything. When I came back to New Orleans, I knew he was scamming and selling drugs. The Coast Guard deals with drug interdiction so it was perfect."

"How did you afford your car?"

"It was a gift from my uncle for the, 'work,' I did. He thought I was useful for information. They say I can keep it. Along with the college money he squandered at present day value. I love what I do, so I'll probably use it for a down payment on a house. Sad how expensive education is these days." He winked at me. He knew, as well as I did, that students going to school in the fine city of New Orleans were paying one hundred and twenty thousand for four years of substance induced stupors.

"I went to see my grandparents this morning to prepare them. Not only has the country lost the war on drugs, but drugs will have taken both of their sons. One by death and one by prison."

"I'm sorry I didn't come to you with everything. I was devastated when I saw you at the docks with those snakes. I felt so betrayed. I thought you were guilty. I still love you."

"I still love you too. I'm sorry the honesty wasn't there on both ends."

Jim, and surprisingly Jackson, had helped me realize that the institution made me who I was today. My heartbeat felt like a metronome on its highest octave, ticking loudly. As I took a final glance in the mirror before walking down the hall to the front door, my mind flashed to my hands on the ground, my knees kneeling, the shadow hovering, coming to swallow. But, I would now make peace. The shadow was about to lift. Fates collision made me comfortable with Jim. Fates collision made us interact and now I knew the reason he came into my life. Fates collision would let us find our way back to each other if it was meant to be.

As I turned to leave and stood across from him, able to reach out and touch his face, I saw in him a reflection. The face created, the face I could now recognize, was actually my own. I saw in him, myself. The new self he helped create by entering my life and teaching me I had survived by myself for all these years. I had a new confidence in myself, rather than a false confidence in someone else. I saw myself divided, my self returned. Myself no longer torn. A big world was waiting for me to discover on my own.

Chapter 23

I sat at an outdoor bar in an undisclosed, tropical paradise, sipping a cocktail like a John Grisham character. Actually, I was vacationing in Cartagena, on Colombia's Caribbean coast. Ironically, I ended up in the country that put cocaine on the American map.

The TV screens in the hotel bar played Katie Couric on *Dateline*. She told of a shocking bust that exposed an undercover drug trafficking and money-laundering business from one of the hottest clubs on Bourbon Street. Next, Stone Phillips sat in the jail with Kevin. I stared at his ugly face on the monitor. "The key was *not* to get addicted. Cause when you get high on your own supply, you lose."

"Asshole." I said out loud. A little too loud, because I felt a man wearing a ball cap across the bar give me a dirty look. On screen, Stone Phillips nodded at Kevin, narrowing his eyes. When the report cut back to him, he said to the audience, "There is an expression in the drug world, if you use, you lose. Kevin Perkins certainly lost." Although cocaine was a stimulant, I thought it quite appropriate the man chronicling the incident had the name *Stone*.

Next on screen on this *Dateline* special (aren't all of their crime shows pitched as "special?"), Black Sevens was shown receiving a new light-up sign on Bourbon Street. It would have been sold on auction under the RICO Act. Instead, Jackson's parents bought it in a very silent auction with Porter. Taco and D.J. Ray-Ray survived.

After leaving Jim's apartment early that morning after the bust, I boarded the streetcar to head back uptown to pack my belongings. At least I didn't have to worry about Darla and Beth being home on Walnut Street.

I sat on the streetcar next to a bunch of little old ladies huddled together chatting. I glanced over to the cause of their gossip and saw they were reading a brochure for a church convention they were headed to. One of the seminar topics the ladies were about to attend was called, 'You're okay, and I'm okay, so why did Jesus die?' I looked out the window and thought of the last four months of sex, drugs and rock and roll. I knew I didn't need religion for peace.

I had decided to call agent Porter and give him one last piece of evidence before I left. I sat on the phone with him as his agent went back into hotel room 22 at the Maison Dupuy and picked up a Gideon's Bible. I heard him say, "She wasn't joking. Got it."

When Beth and Kevin tracked us down and broke into the hotel room, they would have been smart to examine the hollowed-out bible where I had placed the external hard drive. Instead, they took the obvious choice of evidence, the laptop.

I knew I couldn't run through the French Quarter with an external hard drive *and* a Glock in my backpack. Those external hard drives were very heavy in 1999 compared to present day lightweight ones that plug in via USB cable. If Kevin had found the external hard drive and taken it, I still would have given the logbooks as evidence. The video footage was icing on the cake. For *everyone*.

Paul Jansen got life for not one attempted murder, but two when he said on tape that he would have Jim take care of me. His sentence was particularly harsh because I was a federal agent. At least, that's what Porter had concocted.

On the screen, Katie Couric finished reporting that, "the undercover female agent that helped bring the organization down was unavailable for comment." Yes, sometimes even the government plays dirty, but it was for the good of many.

A few years later, I took a flight and sat next to an off duty pilot. We started talking about flight security. He told me a little-known story. A man once tried to rush the cockpit. The other passengers detained him, and he choked to death. The point was that no one knew what he would have done if he had gotten to those pilots. Then, everyone might have been harmed if the plane went down. If you are thinking, let a jury decide, well, they did.

The passengers were found not guilty when the case came before the court on September 17, 2001.

Although Agent Porter concocted the agent story so I didn't have to go into the witness protection program, I told him that I was not ready to join them and train to be a real agent. *Just yet.* Perhaps, in a few years. I needed to be on my own for a while. There was a whole big world waiting for me to discover, and I had accepted another offer.

If I was in *Panama,* you could cue your auditory memory for Van Halen. But since I was in Colombia, think Doyle Dane Bernbach's creation of the fictional character Juan Valdez and his mule Conchita. They appeared in advertisements for the National Federation of Coffee Growers of Colombia to tout pure Columbian coffee.

It wasn't Taco that carved my path to Columbia. Pedro had set me up well. He would return to Colombia after Tulane to run the family coffee business. Another stimulant, yes, but legal. His father was at the top of the National Federation of Coffee Growers. He thought it would be a perfect career move for me to attend the University here and learn another language, which could be useful in the international business world or until I joined Porter.

I was brought back to my new surroundings by a familiar voice from the man across the bar who took off his ball cap. "Long time no see, girl."

I turned around and faced someone I hadn't seen in a few months. "I'd say good to see you G, but you really had me fucked there at the end. Are you following me around the world now? Last I heard, you were suspended from duty for Coked Up 7's."

"Back on a new case. Where else do you go to make sure international drug rules are followed?"

"That was so 20 years ago Cono de nieve." I was just beginning Spanish lessons.

"Una buena. Promesa de decir la verdad."

"Promise to tell the truth?"

"I'm here on Porter's orders. Protect you. Especially since you are in trouble once again."

"What are you talking about?"

Rick G. moved over to the barstool next to mine.

"Well, turns out your classmate's family is using their coffee company to send large quantities of weed candy to California."

"Candy? Wow. That's inventive."

"The coffee beans weigh about the same. Weed candy goes for twenty dollars a pop on the street. They don't melt in shipment because of the air tight containers they ship the beans in. You really should have taken the offer to go to D.C. and been a normal college student in a normal town."

"D.C. is far from normal."

"Well, your next location is the D.C. for pretty people."

"Huh?"

Rick G. pointed at his ball cap that read, 'Dodgers.'

"We need you to go undercover in the States at their receiving location in Los Angeles. It's unclear if your friend's family even knows what's going on. His father is practically retired. But the 90's have brought hard times to coffee farmers. Could be why they turned to an alternative source of income."

"Interesting."

"The best part is, I'll be with you posing as your American boyfriend."

"Ataque al corazón."

"You can still learn Spanish. Half of Los Angeles speaks it. You can finish school at UCLA."

Maybe you'll hear from me again, although, you know what they say about sequels.

To Be Continued